The Passionate Ghost

Sheila Rosalynd Allen

JOVE BOOKS, NEW YORK

All the characters and events portrayed in this work are fictitious.

This Jove Book contains the complete
text of the original hardcover edition.
It has been completely reset in a typeface
designed for easy reading and was printed
from new film.

THE PASSIONATE GHOST

A Jove Book / published by arrangement with
Walker and Company, Inc.

PRINTING HISTORY
Walker and Company, Inc. edition published 1991
Jove edition / August 1993

ISBN: 0-515-11165-1

Jove Books are published by The Berkley Publishing Group,
200 Madison Avenue, New York, New York 10016.
The name "JOVE" and the "J" logo
are trademarks belonging to Jove Publications, Inc.

PRINTED IN THE UNITED STATES OF AMERICA

10 9 8 7 6 5 4 3 2 1

IN PURSUIT OF A GHOST . . .

"He may not be appreciative of our intruding upon his solitude," Marie said as they sat upon a brass-bound trunk staring around the cluttered attic. "Perhaps we should leave well enough alone."

"Since we can't see him, I hardly see how we can be intruding upon his privacy," Hero replied practically. "I wonder what one must do or say to call a ghost?"

"I rather assumed he would just appear. As he did before," Marie explained.

"Hardly likely," Hero said. "I mean why would he?"

"Why did he before?" Marie asked.

"I wish I knew," came a gruff reply.

"Hero? I mean, Mr. Hargrave?"

"Please, I like Hero much better."

"Did you just—by any chance—speak?"

"No," Hero replied.

"Did you . . . hear . . . someone speak?" Marie asked.

"I thought I heard something but—by gad! Do you think it's here?"

"Of course I'm here," Sir Harry the Ghost replied irritably. "And I'm not an it, I'm a he. Which brings me to why *you* are wandering about up here. I have precious little to call my own," he groused, "without you humans trampling about in my last refuge . . ."

Also by Sheila Rosalynd Allen

THE RELUCTANT GHOST
THE MEDDLESOME GHOST
THE HELPFUL GHOST

Sir Harry's books are dedicated,
with love from all her family and friends,
to Elva Fraser.

- 1 -

LADY AGATHA STEADFORD-SMYTH was not given to excessive enthusiasms. Nor, having spent most of her life as the wife of a gambler notorious for both his losses and his light-o'-loves, was she filled with optimism. And yet, with a glorious late summer sun warming her gatehouse garden, it was difficult not to succumb to the beauty of the Dorset day and the good news from across the English Channel which had heartened the entire country.

Finally, and at long last, the horrid French upstart, Napoleon, had been defeated and deported to some distant island named Elba. And, while the war in the New World still raged on, it was sure to end soon.

Lady Agatha was as patriotic as any, but, since Napoleon was vanquished and the war the United States had declared against its former ruler was so very far away, neither seemed as important on this glorious Dorset day as the coming harvests. Each year the harbingers of those harvests were Agatha's roses which bloomed from the top of the Abbey Hill to the gatehouse gardens far below.

Her childhood affection for the beautiful blooms had grown into a lifelong passion, nurtured through her marriage, her tenure as owner of the abbey, and for all the long years after her brother had wrested the abbey from her. Both avocation and solace for Lady Agatha, her roses were a sign to the county's farmers of what their own harvests would bring. And in this year of our Lord, 1814, the abbey roses presaged a bountiful harvest. They blazed splashes of deepest crimson, of scarlet, peach and the most delicate pink from near Steadford Abbey's stone walls down across the greensward to the tiny garden of the small stone gatehouse at the base of the hill where Lady Agatha now lived.

Pleased with her roses, and thinking of the coming harvest, Lady Agatha lifted her attention from the gatehouse flowers. Her hand shielding her eyes from the summer sun, she gazed at the sloping green vistas beyond the neatly clipped gatehouse hedges. The Abbey Hill rose gently upwards from Agatha's vantage point near the ancient arched gateway. Rolling lawns were nearby, a stand of oaks in the distance, and in between, a winding line of copper beeches that followed the narrow road towards the crest of the hill and the abbey itself.

Steadford Abbey stood sentinel at the peak of its own hill, the three-storey mansion commanding a sweeping view of the countryside below and beyond. The ancient stone presence seemed to demand obeisance of its smaller and more commonplace neighbours in the distances beyond the Abbey Hill.

"Aggie?" Fannie Burns asked with worry behind her words as she came from the kitchen doorway. Lady Agatha's abigail for nearly forty years, Fannie spoke in the familiar manner which had long since developed between mistress and servant when they were alone. "Is something amiss?"

Lady Agatha turned her attention from the distances beyond her garden to the pensive look in her abigail's eyes. "What could be amiss?" she asked back.

Fannie was nearly twenty years younger than her mistress and in her early fifties she was still a pretty woman. She lacked Lady Agatha's patrician bones and thick silver-washed black hair but Fannie was sweet-featured and kind, even if a bit sharp-tongued upon occasion, a trait she and her mistress shared. At the moment, Fannie was eyeing that mistress carefully. "With you down here in the gatehouse and none at all living in the abbey itself, would it be a wonder if you thought about the waste of it all? Or worried about what was to become of us?"

A small muscle in Lady Agatha's cheek twitched. Proud of the English tradition of stiff-upper-lip, Agatha could not abide weakness in her fellow females. Having survived her inheritance being stolen by her very own brother, having survived the death of love, innocence and her own children, Agatha Steadford-Smyth was neither weak nor maudlin.

"Fannie Burns, you are altogether too fanciful," came the reply. "I was merely thinking of the abbey."

"Ah ha, you see? I was right."

"You were not right. I was not thinking of the past or of things that can not be. I was thinking I might walk up to the abbey and make sure all is as it should be after the rain last night."

With pursed lips, Fannie Burns turned back to the fat cabbage roses she was cutting for the parlour tables. "Nothing's as it should be when you, the rightful owner, are living in the gatehouse and strangers live in the abbey."

"There are no strangers living in the abbey," Agatha pointed out.

"At present," Fannie replied. "I'm not one to dish up a dead man's sins but if it weren't for your good-for-nothing brother selling it out from under you, there never would have been any strangers living in the abbey."

Lady Agatha raised her hand and turned away. "There is nothing to be gained from dwelling on past wrongs."

"And what about present wrongs? What about the London solicitors who bought the abbey when the Beals left? And then none coming to claim it after all these months. A plentiful waste, if you ask me."

"No one has asked you," Agatha pointed out tartly.

Fannie Burns paid no attention to her mistress's tone of voice. "The keys are on the sideboard," she said as Lady Agatha headed into the gatehouse kitchen.

While Lady Agatha went in search of the abbey keys, two small figures were darting across the abbey grounds.

"Shhh," Jessie Beecher hushed her ten-year-old sister, Dulcie. "Did you hear something?"

Jessie, three years older, was just ahead of Dulcie on the crest of Abbey Hill. When she stopped moving, her younger sister bumped into her.

Dulcie's young eyes were large with growing fright as she stared up at the towering stone building. It seemed to reach all the way to touch the very sky high above their heads. "I think we should j-just g-go home, Jessie."

"Go on then, if you're so afraid, go home," Jessie commanded. "I shan't be scared off."

"You must come too."

"I will not come too! I am not the one who's afraid and you are making me excessively upset, Dulcie Beecher. You can hie yourself off home if you like but I am going to play hide-and-seek inside the castle just as we planned."

"It's not a castle," Dulcie said. "Besides, one can't very well play hide-and-seek alone," she pointed out.

"I shall play hide-and-seek with the abbey ghost," Jessie retorted.

Dulcie's eyes widened. "Oh, Jessie, you never shall! You can't. Papa says all that talk about a ghost is nothing but rubbishy foolishness. There are no such things as ghosts."

"Well I shall know the truth of it and you never shall," Jessie retorted. As she spoke she started forward again. Her young heart hammered against her ribs but she was not going to reveal any fear to her younger sister. Determination was written across her freckled face.

Dulcie moved quickly to catch up with her sister. "You mustn't go in there! Only fancy if you are right and there *is* a ghost." Her voice was full of awe.

Jessie gave an impatient shake of her head but did not stop walking forward. "If there is, I shall see it for myself. There, did you hear that?"

"I heard the wind, I think," Dulcie replied, swallowing.

"No, something else." Jessie stopped to listen.

Dulcie grabbed her sister's arm. "Oh, Jessie, please be careful. Do you suppose Papa could be wrong and there really is a ghost up here?"

"Hush so I can hear."

Dulcie shivered as she followed her sister around the side of the house, staying as close as she could get. The cabbage roses along the west side of the abbey were in full late summer bloom, the sun's warmth releasing their sweet scent into the afternoon breeze. Bees called to feast by the soft fragrances buzzed lazily amongst the blossoms.

Jessie darted around a small swarm of bees, starting around the front of the house and then ducking back beside her sister. "It's Lady Agatha!" Jessie shoved Dulcie between two of the rosebushes, following quickly and crouching down. There might or might not be a ghost but rose thorns and bees were infinitely preferable to earning the venerable Lady Agatha's wrath.

The girls might be the in-laws of the former owner but they had no business in the abbey and Lady Agatha Steadford was known far and wide as a stickler for what was proper and what was not. And young girls sneaking into the abbey looking for ghosts was far from proper.

"Ouch." Dulcie brought a finger to her lips, sucking at where a thorn had grazed it. "I want to go home," she moaned.

"Don't be such a goose," her sister reprimanded in a loud whisper. She crouched low against the old stones, Dulcie huddling close and closing her eyes tight, wishing herself safe home in their tidy flat over her father's butcher shop. If their eldest brother, Paul, hadn't married Becky Beal and taken her to London, Jessie would never have given two thoughts to the abbey. But Becky had to go prattling on about the abbey ghost in the letters she sent to Paul's family and Jessie was cut from the same cloth as Becky Beal, just as Papa said. Both of them too adventurous by half. Becky had ended all right and tight and married proper but she had been all of eighteen and her father had money and had bought the abbey after all.

Tom Beecher had no such money and gave short shrift to such goings-on as girls traipsing about the countryside as if they were farm boys, as he often told his wife. Molly Beecher agreed, but she winked at Jessie's doings and kept her girls out of trouble with their father.

But Molly Beecher would not be able to stem her husband's wrath if Lady Agatha brought them home in disgrace. Dulcie squatted down closer to the sun-warmed abbey stones and closed her eyes tight.

Lady Agatha placed the large iron key in the huge abbey door and unlocked it. The thick iron-banded oak door opened,

revealing the empty main hall and wide oak staircase to the
upper floors.

The only sunlight came from above, where tall, square,
mullioned windows lined the front wall of the Long Gallery high above Lady Agatha's head. Stone-floored, the
hall was cold, the afternoon's summer warmth unable to
penetrate the abbey's thick walls. Drafts of cold stale air
swirled around her ankles, chilling her as she lifted her
skirts and stepped inside.

During his tenure as owner of the abbey, George Beal
had completed the renovations and repairs that Sir Giles
Steadford had begun years before. The rich merchant had
completely refurbished the ancient abbey, its cracks repaired,
its carpets and curtains new. There were even new furnish-
ings in many of the parlours and suites, selected by the
merchant's wife, Mary Beal, who had more liking for the
opulent and the oriental than she had taste. But the huge
house—even with its new finery—was sadder than it had
ever been in the long years of Lady Agatha's stewardship
when, although poor and unrepaired, love and life inhab-
ited its walls. Now it was empty, silent and forlorn.

Lady Agatha paused at the foot of the wide stairwell,
listening to the silence. She debated with herself about
leaving, about turning around and walking back down to
the gatehouse and leaving well enough alone. But even as
she did she castigated herself for being a foolish female and
walked forward down the long hallway.

Closed doors hid the large front parlours, the abbey ballroom and the main dining room. Lady Agatha passed them
all, pausing only when she reached double doors far back
along the hallway.

She opened the doors into the small Tudor chapel but
hesitated again on the threshold. The afternoon sunlight
poured through a round stained-glass window, creating rainbows that fell from the archangel Michael's widespread
arms.

A thick layer of dust had settled on the walnut pews.
More dust motes, unsettled when Lady Agatha opened the
doors, floated upwards on the rainbowed sunbeams. Agatha

looked towards the choir loft and the ancient pipe organ, inwardly hearing its sadly sweet music. Sad, sweet and melancholy music that played only in her memory.

"Are you here?" she whispered, feeling more foolish by the minute. "I am a silly old fool, aren't I?" She seemed to wait for the house itself to answer.

High above in the drafty old house, in the long unused nursery, a strangely clad figure lay atop a long trestle table. The table, well-scarred with the marks of years of children's play, did not look particularly inviting.

In the silent, still room Sir Harry the Ghost suddenly rose straight up from the table. He floated upwards towards the ceiling and then straightened his posture and came downwards, touching his feet to the wood plank flooring. He was dressed in an antique and rather tattered purple coat with buttoned-back revers and cuffs *à la marinière* and skirts much too long for modern dress. A half century before, his costume, if new, would have been the height of fashion for a military man. As it was, it left a great deal to be desired.

"Aggie?" he said, his voice croaking with disuse. "Damn and blast!" he bellowed, the words coming out stronger. "That's better," he told the air around him grumpily before he remembered what had awakened him. "Aggie, are you here?"

He moved towards the hall, his body disappearing through the closed door and then slipping downwards through the floors and ceilings to come to rest in the choir loft above Lady Agatha's head.

"Aye, and I knew it. I knew it was you who woke me, Aggie-my-girl. Can you see me now?" Lady Agatha was looking up at the stained-glass archangel, not at Harry. Sir Harry's hopes dashed, he slumped forward to a seat on the choir loft railing, his long legs dangling over the side.

"I'll warrant none's ever been worse used than I, man or ghost," Sir Harry complained. "I've languished for forty years in this exile between heaven and earth. I've done all I know how and more besides to end this damnable curse,

I've brought Steadfords and any who live here their rightful loves for an entire decade and still my Aggie can't see or hear me! It's more than a body could bear, if one had a proper body. I've no notion what else I can do to make things come out right. There are no Steadfords here for me to marry off. There's *no one* here, let alone any I could marry off, and Aggie, since I'm to make the course of true love run smooth, and I cannot leave the abbey, I've naught to work with if no damnable Steadfords live in the abbey!" He roared the words no one could hear and became more upset by the moment.

"Begging your pardon about the 'damnable,' " he muttered, just in case. "I know my temper's not of the best but I'd like to see any who was calm and collected after suffering such ignominy as I've been dealt for all these years. Left to languish unseen for thirty years and then only seen by lovers these past ten. At least before you caught a glimpse or two of me. I know you did, even if you didn't believe the report your eyes gave you."

His words put an idea in his head and he drifted down towards Lady Agatha, floating a few feet in front of her.

"Mayhap you can see me better if I'm closer. Can you see me now, Aggie?" he questioned.

Lady Agatha sighed and sank to a seat on the front pew.

"Aggie?" he asked hopefully and came nearer, his figure almost transparent in the sunlight.

Lady Agatha was staring upwards at the stained glass. "It seemed so real," she mused out loud. "Of course I must be touched to even consider there might be—you might be—real." She trailed off. "And to keep coming back, as if you would be here. It was so long ago . . . years now . . . I must have dreamt it."

"You did not dream it, you saw me well enough," Harry tried to tell her. "You looked straight at me at the Beal girls' weddings and you heard me playing the organ. Aggie, you heard me, the whole bloody village heard me!"

A very determined Agatha Steadford rose to her feet, brushing her black skirts free of dust and turning towards the door.

"Don't go yet," Harry said, following behind her. "Aggie, you've only just come and I've not seen you for over a month."

Since she could not hear them, his words did no good. He tried to follow her outside but found he could not penetrate the huge oak door that she was closing in his face. "By Jupiter, there must be a way," he thundered, but he was just as frustrated by the outer wall as by the door. "I used to be able to sail straight through these blasted walls." A horrible thought occurred to him, leaving him more agitated than before. What if he were losing his powers? What if he could not make any see or hear him ever again? Would he be forsaken here forever, halfway between life and death, never to earn his freedom?

With such thoughts heavy upon his heart, Sir Harry the Ghost drifted upwards towards the abbey attics.

Lady Agatha paused on the driveway outside, looking out across the summery countryside at the familiar view. "You are becoming a sentimental old fool," she told herself sharply.

"You see?" Jessie breathed the words from her vantage point at the corner of the house. Hidden by the fragrant rosebushes, Dulcie peered over her sister's shoulder, trying to see around the corner of the house. "I told you I heard Lady Agatha talking to someone."

"But nobody's with her," Dulcie objected.

"She's talking to the ghost," Jessie said with authority.

"Where?" Dulcie began to rise, trying to see farther around the corner. Her sister dragged her back down.

"I told you he existed," Jessie said. "Becky said he was as real as real could be and it was him who helped her marry our Paul right in this very house. I'm going inside."

"Are you very sure we should?"

"I'm very sure *I* should," came Jessie's reply. "You can do as you please."

Dulcie pulled a face. "I know what you're after in that house, Jessie Beecher. You are sweet on Tommy Sedgins and Becky said the abbey ghost helped true love and that's why you want to see that old ghost."

"It is not," Jessie answered. But she was already making her way back along the rows of rosebushes to the terrace steps and the doors that led into the ballroom.

Lady Agatha was far off down the drive, her straight-backed figure growing smaller and walking slowly, a walking stick in her hand, a small Norwich shawl made of blue cotton around her shoulders. She did not look back to see the girls sneaking into the abbey through the unlocked terrace door, nor did she hear Harry's continuing tirade.

Neither Jessie nor Dulcie heard Sir Harry's words but they soon began to feel his wrath as words failed him and he resorted to more ghostly means of expression.

The draught in the main hall became a breeze and then a full-fledged, roaring wind rumbling through the halls and up and down the stairwells.

"Do you hear something?" Dulcie asked in faltering tones.

"Just an old house's rumbles. You know how our house creaks and groans."

"Yes, but those are little sounds."

"And our house is a little house. Bigger houses make bigger sounds," Jessie said practically. She would have said more but she was opening the hallway door at the time and never got the chance. A howling wind knocked her backwards into Dulcie. They both tumbled to the floor, their cotton skirts ballooning upwards.

"Jessie," Dulcie shrieked as she grabbed at her skirts and began to cry. "I want to go home," she managed to say betwixt her tears.

Jessie wrestled with her own skirts, her heart hammering just as fiercely as her younger sister's.

Something rushed past them just above their heads. As dark as a storm cloud, it swirled around them, scaring the wits out of the young girls and sending them scrambling for the terrace doors, their shrieks rising shrill and scared on the roaring wind.

"Damn and blast this cursed ghosthood to hell and beyond and back!" Harry was roaring, his emotional agitation creating the wind that rattled the Steadford family portraits in the

Long Gallery and nearly blew out the windowpanes. "By God, Aggie will know I'm here or I'll—" he promised, raising his ghostly fists to heaven. "I'll—" He could think of no worthy threat. "Or else!" he finally roared along with the hurtling winds.

- 2 -

THE NEXT DAY Lady Agatha sat dozing by the window in her gatehouse bedroom. A shawl had slipped from her lap, the vista of rolling hills and huge oaks beyond her window dappled with early afternoon shadows.

Fannie tapped on the open door. "Aggie?" She came into the room, reaching to pick up the fallen shawl. Along with the shawl a packet of yellowed letters surrounded by a fading red riband had fallen into Lady Agatha's sewing basket.

"I'm not asleep," Agatha declared. She reached for the packet of letters.

"You've been reading those old love letters over and over of late, as if you'd never before seen them."

"Nonsense."

"It's not nonsense and well you know it. And the cause of you pining is that lovely abbey house sitting there empty and going to wrack and ruin and well you know that too."

"If you came up here to make a nuisance of yourself you've done an admirable job of it, Fannie Burns. Now you can go back belowstairs and leave me in peace."

"I came up because you have a visitor," Fannie retorted.

"Why didn't you say so?" Lady Agatha sat up and reached to straighten her lace cap. "Who is it?"

"Leticia Merriweather."

At the mention of the loquacious and gossipy widow, Agatha Steadford sat back and lowered her arms from her cap. "I don't want to see her."

"Now, Aggie, I can't very well tell her you're not here when I've just come up to get you. She'd be all over town with the story of you snubbing her."

"At my age I have the right to be as unsociable as I please."

"Mayhap you do, but you've no right to make my life a

misery, snapping people's heads off at the least little thing and making yourself a nuisance around the kitchen. It will do you good to entertain a caller, give you something to do besides get in my way all afternoon."

"Get in your way," Agatha repeated, dumbfounded.

"Yes and you can take out your ire on that poor old soul instead of venting it all on me," Fannie added tartly.

"I've never been so affronted in my entire life. I have the most regular of temperaments and more patience than most. And as for Leticia Merriweather being a poor old soul, you have gone past all reason if you expect that nonsense to wash with me! Just go right down and tell her I shall not see her."

Fannie made a sound that was not translatable into words but carried with it a very obvious degree of irritation.

"You'll only make your job worse," Agatha said primly, "if you put it off."

"I suppose you've the right of it," Fannie seemed to agree. Her tone was mild. "She'll of course spread word of your indisposition, but that can't be helped."

"What indisposition?" Agatha demanded.

Fannie looked to be the soul of innocence. "Why the one you must have that keeps you to your bed and unable to receive visitors."

"Fannie Burns, you are managing me and I must tell you I do not like it above the half," Agatha declared, her dark eyes alight with anger. "However," she conceded with none too good a grace, "Leticia's gossiping tongue might just do as you say." With that, Lady Agatha got to her feet. However, she gave her serving-woman a withering look before marching past her and into the tiny upstairs hall.

Fannie kept her thoughts to herself. If a self-satisfied little smile curled the edges of her thin lips Lady Agatha did not notice and it was gone before Fannie descended the stairs behind her mistress.

"My dear, dear Lady Agatha," Leticia Merriweather was simpering in the front parlour, "I didn't disturb your rest, did I? I do so hope you are feeling quite the thing?"

Fannie continued towards the kitchen, preparing tea and

biscuits for the visitor whilst Lady Agatha gave short shrift to the widow's questions.

"I've never felt better in my life," Agatha said with more asperity than Leticia's question required. "Never!" she added for emphasis. "Wherever did you find that dress?" Agatha asked once she took a good look at her guest.

Leticia Merriweather was pleased with the question. She made a little half-turn so that Lady Agatha could better see the article of clothing in question. What Lady Agatha saw was a round little dumpling of a woman who seemed to be poured most alarmingly into a straight-skirted, high-waisted dress much too form-fitting and fussy for its occupant.

"Do you like it?"

"No. What color is that called?"

Leticia Merriweather's round little face drooped. "It's called sea's foam, it's all the rage, I assure you. It's the very latest in fashion."

"I've never been one to bow to the changing fashions," Agatha said.

"One can see that," the plump widow murmured, lowering her eyes for a moment before she met the dowager's own and spoke again. "I've brought your post from the village so that poor Fannie would be saved the trip."

"How kind of you," Lady Agatha replied with barely repressed sarcasm. Letty Merriweather merely wanted to be on hand so as to hear the latest *on dits* from London and far-off America. Lady Agatha's granddaughter and family seemed to be safe in the wild west of the Louisiana territories, even with the war being waged by the upstart Americans against their English betters. But Leticia Merriweather loved to be the first with the very latest news and gossip and one could always hope that something perfectly dreadful had happened since Jane's last letter to her grandmother. Of course not to the dear girl herself, or her darling children or the duke, her husband.

Then again, if Leticia had the latest in London gossip at her disposal, thanks to Lady Agatha's young cousin Sir Giles and his very lovely and very social wife, Elizabeth, the widow Merriweather could dine out for weeks upon the juicy tidbits. The stories that were whispered behind fans at Almack's were as much prized in the countryside as they were in London's parlours. And far more picked over as there was so little else for one to do in the countryside.

"I'm quite positive you must be most anxious to hear of your family news. You must not stand on ceremony, dear Lady Agatha. Just forget I am here and I shall be quiet as a tiny mouse while you read." As she spoke Fannie came through the parlour door, carrying the tea tray. "Ah, just the thing, Fannie. And my favourite tea-cakes, how kind."

Fannie gave the woman a brief smile. She had never served a cake the widow Merriweather did not declare as her favourite nor did Fannie calculate she was likely to live long enough to find such a one.

"Go on, dear Lady Agatha, please open your letters and read on. I shall be as quiet as if I were not here," Leticia promised.

"I wouldn't dream of such a breach of etiquette," Lady Agatha said flatly.

Her disappointed guest thought of arguing but knew from long acquaintance how firmly her hostess held to her resolves. "Well, if you're quite sure, I suppose there's nothing to be said to persuade you otherwise." Letty made the feeble attempt but, finding no success, she sighed and helped herself to another cake, making the best of it.

"Have you heard of our new neighbour, Captain Tompkins, Lady Agatha? Such a fine figure of a man and a gentleman farmer. A widower, with grown children into the bargain. Quite, quite eligible and such a shame our social life is so remiss here in the country since the abbey is closed up. What a catch he would be for the Summerville girl or some such."

"A captain?" Fannie put in as she sat down across from Leticia in the small parlour. "Not young, then. Probably much too old for Charlotte Summerville. Or did you mean her mother?"

Leticia laughed. "Fannie Burns, you are such a jester and all of us know it, so I pay you no mind. I spoke up, quite boldly I might say. It was last Sunday at church and

everyone missed you both. I told everyone there had to be
a very good reason you were not coming to church. There
is nothing truly amiss, I hope."

"Your hopes are well-founded," Lady Agatha replied
sharply.

"The weather was unseasonably wet," Fannie said in a
more conciliatory tone.

"Yes, well, in any event, Captain Tompkins is quite, quite
eligible, I assure you."

"Since I have no spinster daughters to marry off, I need
no such assurances," Lady Agatha told the busybody.

Leticia ignored Lady Agatha's dismissive tone. "A true
gentleman, he is, and quite good-looking too, in a distin-
guished sort of way, mind."

Fannie grimaced. "Which means he is grey and over-
weight to boot."

"Not a bit of it," Letty defended. "Well, perhaps a mite
portly. But he carries himself as the soldier he was. Come
to think of it, dear Lady Agatha, it's been some three weeks
since we've seen you in church."

"Do you count the time?" Lady Agatha asked.

Leticia laughed, a merry little peal of self-consciousness.
"How you do put things. But you are being very naughty
and you have not answered me."

"I wasn't aware this was an inquisition," Agatha responded lightly. "We had a touch of the cold," she ended in
dismissive accents that brooked no reply from a sensitive
person.

"Ah, a summer cold," Leticia responded. "They can be
most dangerous, as I'm sure you are aware."

"I am," Agatha replied succinctly.

"You must be sure to take care of a summer cold," Leticia
said as if she were the first with this news.

Unable to withstand more nonsense, Lady Agatha rose to
her feet. "As you say, we must take care of our health. I,
for one, propose to take an afternoon nap. So kind of you
to drop in, Letty. Fannie will see you out." And, with that,
Lady Agatha left the parlour, leaving Fannie to entertain
their astounded guest.

Taken aback by Agatha's sudden departure, Leticia Merriweather looked quite shocked. "I hope I said nothing to distress her ladyship."

"I hardly think you could," Fannie replied. "More tea?" she offered after a silent moment. "Of course, I really should go up and look in upon my mistress."

"And I suppose I should be on my way," the widow said, very obviously disappointed at having to leave without any new gossip.

With more alacrity than was seemly, Fannie saw Leticia Merriweather to the door and closed it firmly behind the little woman's back.

Upstairs Agatha turned on Fannie's approach. Her eyes alight with love and expectation, she held out one of the letters Letty had brought. "Fannie, you will never guess. Jane writes she's coming for my birthday—she's coming home!"

"Never! When?" Fannie took the letter, reading quickly. "The lot of them are coming, fancy that. We'll see the great-grandchildren finally. And she's written to Cousin Giles and Elizabeth to come too if the second baby has arrived." Fannie's practical nature intervened. "Where on earth will we put them all?"

"She says they shall take lodgings nearby," Agatha responded.

Fannie shook her head. "The last of the Steadfords coming home and you not in the abbey. What's to become of this world, I ask you? Wait until Letty Merriweather hears of this."

Agatha grimaced. "There is nothing that goes in that woman's ears that does not pour out her mouth at first opportunity." She opened the second letter, reading it as Fannie read more slowly through Jane's longer letter. "Alice Beal—Lady Andrew I should say—reports the countess is beginning to bend a bit towards her."

"Finally," Fannie replied. "It's the baby girl that did it. One look at her granddaughter and she could hold out no longer, I'll warrant."

"They've named her Agatha," Lady Agatha said with more than a little pride.

"As well they should," Fannie replied. "Do you realise, what with Jane's little Agatha and Elizabeth naming their first one after you, Alice's makes three little Aggies running about?"

"And I hope they have more luck at life's joys than their namesake did."

"Ah, Aggie." Fannie folded Jane's letter, looking towards her employer with true concern. "Are you quite sure you're feeling well? You sounded so—strange—just then."

"Strange, is it?" Agatha asked, rallying. "Don't you start nattering on about my health or I shall be vexed beyond words. I've had enough of that for one day. I'll warrant I'm a bit tired, but that's to be expected after dealing with the likes of Letty Merriweather. She would try the patience of a saint. A bit of a nap will fix me up fine."

"I suppose I'd best leave you to it then," Fannie replied.

"Yes." As Fannie left the room her mistress called out to her. "I'm thinking of sending to those London solicitors who bought the abbey. Since none are living there, they might allow us to use the abbey for a fortnight or so. When Jane and the children arrive."

"What a grand idea," Fannie said before she closed the bedroom door.

Inside the bedroom, Agatha refolded the new letters and placed them on her night table to reread later. She glanced towards her chair by the window but decided to lie down instead.

There was a thin coverlet on the bed. Agatha drew it around herself as she lay back upon her pillows and reached for the red-ribanded packet of ancient letters, holding them close as she closed her eyes.

It was 1761 again. As real as real could be. She could see herself at eighteen, she could see Harry standing before her in the abbey woods, tethering his favourite chestnut stallion. The grounds were white with iced-over snow that crackled beneath their feet and piled up on the bare tree branches around the roots of the huge old trees.

Henry Daniel George Aldworth, Baronet, was twenty years old and dressed in a bottle green frock coat, plain except for the black braid at shoulders and cuffs. With his black knee breeches, black military jackboots and black greatcoat thrown back across his shoulders, he was the most magnificent of men. He turned towards her and she realised he wore no powdered wig. His bicorne riding hat rested atop his own naturally dark, curly hair.

"I came the first moment I could," he said as he turned to face the dark-haired beauty who, wrapped in coat and shawls, was staring at him, totally out of countenance. "Aggie, what is it? What's wrong?" He came near to grab her hands, towering over her, concern writ large across his handsome features. "What's happened?"

"Sir, you are undressed," the young Agatha said, so taken aback by his wigless state she blushed.

"Oh, that." He dismissed the subject with a wave of his hand. "Giles and Edgar and your most humble and obedient servant," he made a sweeping bow, "have made a pact, since we are to be military men, to forswear the use of all such fripperies and fopperies." He spoke of his best friends. "What say you, my sweet, have I need of such embellishments?"

Agatha cast him a very speaking look from beneath long, dark lashes. "I think you have very little need of any thing at all save yourself, sir."

Harry laughed and grabbed her about the waist. "Now that's what a man likes to hear but it's not true, for I need you like the very devil and I shall have you too."

"Harry! You must let me go at once," she said with much more propriety than conviction. "Papa said I am not to allow your addresses. He says you are too ramshackle by half and he's not even seen you without your wig. I don't know what he will say about that."

"More fustian, no doubt."

"If he were here to see us right this minute, he would mill you down!"

"Mill me down, would he?" Harry held Agatha closer

and kissed her soundly. "And what would he do about that, my love?"

"Run you through," Agatha replied gaily.

"Ah ha, and you laughing at my demise, I can see it all plain as plain. Well, I'd best count myself lucky he's not here to see us then, shan't I, for you, my girl, are going to give me many another kiss from those sweet lips before I let you go."

Agatha twisted her head to the side, away from his kisses, giggling as he bent to recapture her mouth. "You are the most frightfully undressed and terribly unmannered gentleman in all of England!"

"And when our new King George sends me off to fight the heathen Indians in the New World will you be thinking of my clothes and my manners, Aggie-my-girl? Or will you be thinking of this, mayhap?" He drew her closer, his hand reaching to tip her chin back, trailing kisses across her cheeks and eyes. Her contented little sigh warmed his heart. "I shall speak to your father this very day," he whispered into her ear.

Fannie tiptoed into the gatehouse bedroom. Lady Agatha was sleeping, her expression serene. A soft smile played across her slumbering face, and Fannie hated to wake her from her dreams.

"Aggie—" Fannie touched Lady Agatha's shoulder lightly as she spoke her name.

Agatha heard Harry calling her name, her dream coming true as she opened her eyes, still smiling, and found the serving-woman standing over her. Agatha blinked, looking a bit confused.

"Aggie, are you all right?"

". . . Yes."

"I didn't want to wake you, but someone's come about the abbey. And without sending word they were coming, mind." Fannie reached to help Lady Agatha but her help was impatiently brushed aside.

"Stop fussing about," Agatha said.

"I don't know what the world is coming to, no manners

at all if you ask me. I told the driver they'd best wait in the coach." Fannie reached for her mistress's blue silk shawl.

"I don't need my shawl."

"There's a bit of a chill in the afternoon air and you don't want another summer cold," Fannie responded firmly as she placed the shawl firmly upon Lady Agatha's thin shoulders.

With a grimace that spoke volumes, Lady Agatha accepted the shawl and descended to greet the unexpected visitors. Fannie hurried ahead to inform the coachman her ladyship was ready to receive his passengers.

Lady Agatha settled into her favourite wing chair in the small gatehouse parlour, glancing out the window in time to see two women coming up the path from the garden gate. Soon she heard voices in the tiny hall and Fannie appeared in the doorway, followed by a stern-faced woman of middling years. The woman saw Lady Agatha and came forward.

"I believe you are expecting our arrival, Lady Agatha. I am Delia Dutton and this is my mistress, Miss Marie Angelique Aldworth, Major Aldworth's daughter."

Delia Dutton glanced towards her beautiful young mistress as she spoke and so did not see Agatha Steadford as the expression of polite interest drained from her face. Shocked, Agatha stared up at the dark-haired beauty who took a tentative step forward, her expression diffident as she gave a small curtsey to the elderly dowager.

"I am terribly sorry if we are inconveniencing you, Lady Agatha." The timbre of her voice was low, the tone melodious. Seeing the older woman's confused expression and realising the redoubtable dowager had given no reply, Marie Aldworth spoke more slowly, carefully enunciating each word. "My father has recently acquired the abbey and we have come ahead to ensure all will be in readiness for his arrival. We have only just arrived from the continent, my abigail and myself, and were told you were in possession of the keys."

Fannie saw her mistress's distressed expression and came forward, worried. "Lady Agatha?"

The old woman did not hear Fannie call her name; she did not turn her eyes from the young beauty who stood before her.

"Did you say Aldworth?" Lady Agatha asked faintly.

"It's a common enough name," Fannie put in quickly, afraid her mistress would say more and betray herself.

"Common!" Delia Dutton was affronted at the slight to her employer's family name.

"Surely my father's solicitors sent word to expect our arrival," Marie said.

Delia Dutton dismissed Fannie with one acid glance and then glared at the sight of Lady Agatha's preoccupied expression. "Is something amiss here? Aldworth is a worthy name, I assure you," she said in frosty accents. "Major Aldworth is a respected member of the duke's staff and is renowned for both his valour and his diplomatic skills."

With great effort Lady Agatha drew herself together, masking her confused emotions under a strained but polite smile. "Please forgive me, but we have received no word of your coming."

"It is we who should apologise if we have descended upon you unannounced, Lady Agatha. We were assured we would be expected. We were told that you were the custodian of the abbey whilst it was unoccupied and that the keys would await us at the abbey gatehouse. I do hope this is the case, since we are quite done up."

"The keys, yes, of course." She looked towards her servingwoman. "Fannie, please fetch the keys for Miss— Miss Aldworth." Agatha stumbled over the name.

Fannie Burns hesitated and then decided against the words she was about to speak. She left the parlour as Lady Agatha offered the young woman tea.

"We have no wish to impose upon you further," Marie replied.

"Since we shall be close neighbours, I hope there will be no need for us to stand upon great ceremony," Lady Agatha said. Curiosity was alight in her eyes as she smiled up at the lovely young miss. "The abbey will be woefully cold until the fires are lit. It is lacking house servants, and supplies as well, since we had no prior word of your arrival. If you will permit me, I shall have Fannie bring a light tea for you both." She included Delia Dutton in her invitation.

Fannie came back into the parlour carrying a tea tray. Delia Dutton put her hand out for the keys she saw on the silver serving tray but Fannie moved on past the woman. Fannie set the tray on a delicate Queen Anne table beside Lady Agatha, fussing with the tea and cakes before handing the abbey keys to Lady Agatha.

"You are much too kind," Marie said.

"Nonsense. Fannie, you'd best go across to the stables and tell young Tim or Homer to unlock the abbey and help the hired coachman unload the luggage."

"I shall unlock the abbey," Delia Dutton told the room.

Lady Agatha hesitated a fraction of a moment and then with good grace handed the keys over to the very determined abigail. "If you wish."

"Delia," Marie put in, "you must be quite as famished as I."

"I know my duty and I have never shirked it, no matter the personal cost," the sour-faced woman replied smugly. "There are certain boxes that must be delicately treated."

"There is no need for worry about your boxes," Fannie told the unfriendly female.

"I must see to paying for the hired coach," Delia insisted. She followed Fannie out, leaving Marie Aldworth and Agatha Steadford-Smyth to their tea and cakes.

3

MARIE ALDWORTH SAT across from Lady Agatha in the cosy gatehouse parlour, the afternoon sunlight streaming in at the small-paned windows to warm the fat ruby and crimson roses on the table between them. The young newcomer sat on the edge of her chair, her hands folded primly on her lap. She wore a conservative carriage-dress of pomona green silk topped by a white and green striped spencer, her dark hair piled high beneath a matching bonnet. The rigours of her travel smudged her dark eyes with fatigue which Lady Agatha saw.

"If we had known you were arriving I would have laid in a few staples and seen to airing out the house and hiring a temporary staff. If you wish I can send Tim to the village for a few supplies although I fear it may be impossible to find help today, on such short notice."

"Thank you, we need very little, Lady Agatha. With my father's career sending us all over the continent, and Delia and I forever striving to make our temporary quarters homelike, we are grateful to be able at last to have a true home of our very own. It is we who should apologise for descending upon you without notice. We thought it would be many more months before my father could resign his commission but the battle of Toulouse thankfully has changed all that. Papa decided we should come ahead whilst he completed his last duties. We were to settle his accounts with his solicitors in London and collect the sale papers and the abbey keys. When they informed us the keys were at the abbey gatehouse with the former owner they assured us they would send ahead to warn you of our arrival."

Lady Agatha watched her guest carefully as she spoke. "Am I to understand you have travelled extensively with your father?"

"Oh, yes. Since I was very small."

"It would seem an irregular childhood for a well-brought-up young woman, following an army officer from posting to posting, as well as possibly dangerous," Lady Agatha said.

Marie Aldworth seemed to take umbrage at the former owner's words. "I assure you," she replied stiffly, "my father is the most attentive and punctilious of parents. He would never subject me to hazard or peril." Remembering their rapid departure from the Spanish peninsula, Marie felt a twinge of guilt at her prevarication. Her posture stiffened in defence of her father who could hardly have foretold Boney's battle strategies and had, in any event, kept her safe from harm.

"I meant no disrespect," Lady Agatha said politely. "Indeed, for your father's own peace of mind, I would have thought your relatives would have made you a home here in England instead of subjecting you to such an unsettled existence."

Marie was courteous but still defensive. "We lost my mother when I was very small and we have no other relatives."

"No other relatives? Are you quite sure?" Lady Agatha asked boldly and then amended her words. "I do not mean to be impertinent but I had assumed your father bought the abbey because of its proximity to your Aldworth relations."

Marie looked perplexed. "I am not aware of any Aldworth relations. My father once told me he was an orphan as my mother had been, that they two had been the world and all to each other until I was born. He has told me many times I was his only family."

Lady Agatha's eyes seemed to look forward, as if contemplating other matters entirely. "What a strange coincidence," she murmured.

"I beg your pardon?"

Agatha roused herself and gave the girl a faint smile. "Forgive me, my mind has a tendency to wander of late."

Marie rose from her chair. "I must apologise for taking up so much of your time."

"Not at all." Lady Agatha reached for her lacquered cane, Marie coming forward to assist the older woman to her feet. "Thank you," Lady Agatha said. "If there is any help you need, I hope you won't hesitate to call."

"That is very kind of you."

"You are quite sure you wish to spend the night in the abbey? You are more than welcome to stay here until we can assemble a staff."

"No," Marie replied. "I have looked forward to a home of our own for so very long any small inconveniences will not matter in the least."

"Please," the dowager said. She touched the younger woman's arm, a look of supplication in her eyes. "I fear you were distressed by my questions but I assure you, I meant nothing by them. You see"—Agatha paused, her next words coming very slowly—"I was once acquainted with an Aldworth family that lived here in Dorset."

"I see," Marie said, but in truth she was more confused than ever by the former owner of the abbey.

"At first I hoped—that is, I thought, you might be related to them," Lady Agatha continued. She seemed wistful. "Of course, that isn't possible. The last Aldworth died over forty years ago. It was just that for a moment—" She broke off her words, looking confused and more than a little embarrassed. "It was foolish of me," she ended briskly. "I realise that now. But I would consider it a very great favour if you would allow us to help you settle in, in some small way."

Marie smiled. "Because of your former friends?"

"Because of my former . . . friends."

"I've been told the abbey is a vast establishment," Marie replied. "It would save us a great deal of time if you or your servant could spare a moment to show us where things are kept and such."

"We shall arrive by midmorning," Lady Agatha promised.

"Thank you," Marie replied. "The size of the establishment was a surprise to me," she confided, her naturally sunny disposition thawing her initial unease with the elderly dowager. Marie decided Lady Agatha's earlier remarks were due to the forgetful vagaries and sudden crochets of advancing age and put them behind her, determined to make friends with the woman who would be their nearest neighbour. "I had no idea Papa planned on retiring to anything so grand as Steadford Abbey. I'm afraid we shall rattle about like three peas in a very large pod, at least until I marry."

"Perhaps your father is looking forward to your raising a family there."

"Aye, knowing the way of his mind. It's very like him to plan out the lives of all those around. You'd best have a care or he'll soon be ordering you about too." She saw Lady Agatha's startled expression and laughed. "You have no idea what it is like to live with a military man. I assure you, he has been a commander for such a long time that he is firmly convinced he must take charge of us all. He will be most unhappy if he has no minions to order about."

Lady Agatha grimaced. "I have never met one of their gender who was not an autocrat from the cradle onwards."

"Oh, dear. Then I fear we must blame ourselves," Marie said gaily.

Her words were met with a frown. "I beg your pardon?"

"If the male of the species is thus from the cradle onwards, as you say, we must shoulder the responsibility. It is, after all, we females who raise them up. We must have special care to temper such tendencies early, must we not?" Marie spoke merrily. "I should ever so much dislike having my own sons treat me with the same condescension my father shows. Of course one's father has the right and the obligation to direct one's life, but I must tell you he thinks me the rebel because I own that I do not like it above the half. He says my future husband will have quite a handful and I'm very afraid he has the right of it. For I do so dislike being told what to do, no matter how kind the manner. I have a perfectly good understanding of things and am very well able to direct my own life."

Lady Agatha was of two minds concerning the young woman's words. Agatha had spent her life away from the company of men in order to direct her own affairs but she was of the opinion that very few females had the same capacities for honesty, hard work and plain speech.

"I have shocked you to the core," Marie said into the small silence that followed her former words.

"Not a bit of it," Agatha responded. "I have lived to an advanced age by my own wits."

"Ah, a kindred soul," Marie exclaimed. "In the coming winter months we shall keep ourselves occupied by having great talks about all manner of things, shall we not?"

Lady Agatha smiled in spite of herself at the girl's youthful enthusiasm. The young Marie reminded Lady Agatha of someone she could not quite place. "Yes, of course," she replied.

"Wonderful! Now I must take up no more of your afternoon. Besides, Delia will be needing my help by now." Marie walked with Lady Agatha to the gatehouse door, thanking her again and planning the time they would meet on the morrow.

Fannie came down the garden path a few minutes after Marie Aldworth left, telling tales of the redoubtable Delia Dutton. "A rare one, she is, I can tell you that," Fannie said. "Thinks she knows it all and more besides. If you ask me she's just a mite too full of herself, that one. Says as how she's been all over the world, she has and knows it all. I put in about Jane being in America and got shut of her chatter good and quick."

"The girl is very nice," Lady Agatha said.

"She seems a good enough sort," Fannie agreed. "Although rambling about the continent all her life is hardly a good upbringing for a proper young miss. Then again, I suppose foreign girls are raised differently."

"Foreign?"

"Her mother was Belgian, Miss Dutton told me. Orphaned and befriended by some English family living abroad. What times we live in, with young girls having to fend for themselves. Do you suppose they're related to the Dorset Aldworths?"

"No, she says not," Agatha replied. "She couldn't be," Agatha continued in a firmer tone.

Fannie hesitated. "Perhaps Henry Aldworth married."

"No, he never did," Agatha answered and then she stared at her abigail. "What do you know of Henry Aldworth?"

"Aggie, when Daniel was killed in the war, I was the one who nursed you through all those days of delirium."

"You never said I spoke about—about the past."

"I was only sixteen then."

"But you've never said anything since."

"And what would be the reason to remind you of old hurts?"

"What did I say?"

"You thought you were telling Henry Aldworth about—about what had happened."

Lady Agatha paled. "Good Lord . . ."

"None heard you but me. I wouldn't let them near. I only spoke of it now because I saw the start the girl gave you when she said her name."

"I can't place where, but it seems as if I've seen her before," Agatha explained.

"You have. In the mirror. The girl is the spitting image of you."

"Me!" Agatha's dark eyes widened.

"And who else?" Fannie asked. "With all that mass of dark hair and those dark eyes so black they look as if tears were captured inside and the skin as fair as ivory. I don't know which is more peculiar, young Marie looking so like you or her being named Aldworth, but I think the Good Lord is having the final say in it all."

"I don't know what you mean."

"Aggie, all the village is saying it's more than passing strange that after all the bad blood between your father and the Aldworths, here come Aldworths to own Steadford Abbey itself, and they don't know the half of it."

"It's not the same family I tell you."

"Same or no," Fannie said, "they're Aldworths and they own the abbey. It's a miracle of God's justice."

"Perhaps merely poetic justice," Agatha mused sadly, more to herself than to her listener.

Up at the abbey the afternoon was slipping into twilight as young Tim and the elderly Homer finished removing the parcels, packages, boxes and trunks from the abbey's entrance court. Carrying, trundling and pushing, together and separately, they managed to convey the baggage into the abbey and even take some of it up the grand staircase.

"That's as much as can be done this day," Homer told his assistant. "You'd best get back to the stable and see to Bess." He spoke of a mare who was about to foal. Young Tim, who had reached his early twenties still being called by his childhood nickname, touched his cap and took off on foot, leaving the cart for Homer.

Delia Dutton bustled about, inspecting the boxes to ensure naught had been broken or damaged and clucking at Homer's rather offhand approach to Marie's possessions. "My good man, if you can't manage a gentle touch, you'd best leave the rest to me."

Homer took her at her word and straightened up. "It's all rug with me," he told her truthfully. "I'd as soon be off."

"Just wait a minute there," the serving-woman called as he started down the wide hallway towards the green baize door that led to the kitchens. "You must show me where the candles are before you go."

"Aye, and what do you think I'm about?" Homer asked crossly. "Come along then, I've me own chores to worrit over."

"I'll come," Marie told him from above. She spoke as she came down the wide mahogany stairs from an inspection of the upper floor.

"I shall see to it," Delia responded.

"Then we both shall," Marie insisted. "I've done little enough as it is and I'm sorry, but I found a long gallery above with the most amazing portraits, one more beautiful than the next." She saw the stableman's odd expression and stopped. "Is something wrong?"

The old man was taking his first long look at the young woman.

"It's Homer, isn't it?" Marie asked.

"Yes, miss, and I'm sorry if I be staring but there it is."

"There is what?" Delia put in.

"If you'd known her then, you'd swear she was back as she was, may I be struck in the nitch if it's not the truth!"

"I beg your pardon?" Marie said.

Homer reacted as if they doubted him. He looked from the prune-faced spinster to the young beauty. "Just go look for yourself at her portrait, and you'll see with your very own eyes."

"My good man," Delia interjected, "we haven't the least idea what you are saying."

"I'm not your good man," Homer told the serving-woman. "And I'm not dicked in the nob," he informed the abbey's new mistress. "If you go look at our Lady Agatha's very own portrait, you'll see for yourself." So saying, he started away.

"And where are you going?" Delia demanded.

"To see to your lamps so you'll not be in the dark this night and thence to lay a fire in your chamber and thence to my fireside to some peace and quiet away from hard-tongued females."

"How dare you," Delia exclaimed. "You are speaking in the presence of your new mistress!"

"Delia—" Marie remonstrated but Homer answered the abigail.

"And well I know it, since you've prattled naught else in my ears these hours past," he told the woman.

"You'd best have a care," she warned. "I've never heard of a servant speaking in such tones to his employer." She sniffed. "And you cannot claim ignorance and excuse yourself on that head."

"Nor would I," Homer retorted. "Nor have I ever spoken disrespectful to my employers," he told her flatly. "I was speaking of yourself."

"Of all the insufferable men I have ever met, you are the worst. I've never been so insulted in my entire life!"

"I misdoubt that," Homer replied.

"Miss Marie, have you heard the temerity—" Delia Dutton turned towards her mistress as she spoke but Marie was not there. "Miss Marie?"

"Most like she's gone to look for candles," Homer said, the light in the great hall growing ever dimmer. "At least she's one that knows how to do something useful." The green baize door banged shut behind him, punctuating his terse words.

He left behind a baleful-eyed abigail who decided then and there that if she had anything to do with it the stable-man was not long for her mistress's employ. Determined to have a very great deal to do with it, Delia Dutton mentally girded her loins for battle and sailed through the green baize door.

Down the servants' hall in the kitchen she found only Marie. "Where is that odious man?"

"I sent him up to lay on a fire for us and then home to his supper," Marie replied mildly.

Grim lines etched the abigail's face. "You must start out with servants as you mean to go on, Miss Marie. If you allow impertinence from one, you shall receive it from all," she said emphatically.

Marie looked up from the lamp she was lighting, an amused sparkle in her eyes. "Then I must be most careful with my abigail, mustn't I?"

Delia Dutton's eyes opened wide in surprise. She opened her mouth and then clamped it shut, her lips compressing into a thin, disapproving line.

"Delia?" Marie smiled at the woman who had raised her. "Have you now lost all sense of humour?"

"I see nothing humourous in being unfairly castigated," the older woman said repressively.

"Nor have you been."

"You did not hear all that—that *stableman*—said to me!"

"Delia, none were expecting our arrival, we took him from his normal chores and made him cart heavy boxes for hours when one can see he is much too old for that sort of thing. He was tired and hungry and crotchety and so you and I would be in the same circumstances."

"You are much too lenient. I fear what a sad coil you shall make treating servants as equals."

Marie gave her abigail a small smile. "How could I do less when you are my servant?"

Delia, caught between fondness and reproach, could think of no proper reply. A resounding thud invaded the stillness, startling them both. Delia gave a little start, straightening and looking towards the servants' hallway.

"What was that?"

"Homer, most probably," Marie answered.

"Someone must tell him not to go about banging doors shut," Delia said, but a strange expression played about her features.

"Is something wrong?" Marie asked.

Delia looked embarrassed. "What? No, of course not."

"You look frightened."

"Nonsense," Delia said with more conviction than she truly felt. The unknown house loomed dark and forbidding beyond the flickering light from the two kitchen lamps Homer had lit before he went above with the coal scuttle.

Marie gave a little laugh. "You look as if you were expecting ghosts."

"Did Lady Agatha tell you then?" Delia queried, her eyes large.

"Tell me what?"

"Of the abbey ghost."

"Delia Dutton, what foolishness are you talking about?"

"The one they call Young Tim asked if we were staying alone in the abbey this night and when I said we were he said he never would. He said the abbey ghost cannot abide strangers and when he walks at night it's a fearful amount of noise as will surely keep one up all night. And the sight of him could put one in their grave."

"Stuff and nonsense," Marie replied, "he was gammoning you and you took him seriously."

"He was as serious as death," Delia defended.

"And so now you believe in ghosties and goblins?" Marie scoffed.

Provoked by Marie's disbelief, her abigail spoke sharply. "Before this night is out you may rue your skepticism." She spoke to her mistress's back as Marie, with lamp in hand, searched the empty cupboards.

"What I shall surely rue," Marie replied, "is an empty stomach unless we can find something more than this." She held the lamp in one hand and a lone glass jar filled with plums from the abbey trees in the other. "I fear the abbey cupboards are as bare as Lady Agatha said. I hope there is something left in our travelling basket or you shall not have to worry about ghosts keeping you awake. If you hear rumbling and groaning it shall be my stomach, not any goblins or ghosts."

Delia reached for the oil lamp on the rough-hewn kitchen table and brought it near the wicker basket that contained the last of their travelling sustenance. "Laugh as you like, he who laughs last, laughs best," she said as she rummaged in the wicker hamper.

"Have you found anything for us?" Marie asked as her abigail emptied the basket of food.

"There's bread and cheese and a bit of chicken."

"Wonderful! I shall put some water on the fire for tea and we shall eat in our chambers, what do you say?"

"Whatever you wish," Delia replied, reproach in every syllable.

"Come along," Marie cajoled. "We shall be warm and cosy and entirely safe. You shall see. And tomorrow we shall begin to make this old ruin a proper home."

Delia grimaced. "How we are to accomplish such an impossibility I haven't the least notion. I don't scruple to say I misdoubt anyone could turn this dusty echo-filled cavern into a proper home."

"It will look much better to you in the morning light, ghosts and all," Marie replied saucily.

Delia pursed her lips, one eyebrow rising in quizzical disdain. "Have I ever mentioned that your perennial optimism is most odiously provoking?"

Marie smiled. "Often and often. Young Tim brought up a bottle of sherry from Lady Agatha so we shall dine like queens and retire to our bedchambers sated and content."

"Chambers?" Delia heard only the one word. The thought of sleeping alone in an unfamiliar bed, in the midst of the cavernous and inky-dark house, did not sit well. Delia Dutton was not of a superstitious nature but the abbey had an unsettling effect on her. "I rather thought we would share a room this night," she said in what she hoped were diffident tones. "I knew you would not want to be alone, the house being so strange and so large."

Marie bit the inside of her lower lip so as to keep from smiling. "What a good idea," she finally managed to reply. "I should be glad of the company."

"Yes, well, I thought as much," Delia answered, her relief apparent in every syllable.

But hours later it was Marie whose sleep was interrupted by troubled dreams. It was in the wee hours just before dawn that her eyes opened, the unfamiliar room alien and cold, despite the fire in the grate and the soft steady snoring from Delia's narrow bed across the large room.

Nothing was amiss and yet something seemed to intrude upon her ease of mind. She could not place what it was nor did she see the incredible apparition that hovered in the air very near the ornately carved walnut bed upon which she lay.

"So you're the one who disturbed my rest," Sir Harry the Ghost said in acerbic accents. He looked more closely at the young woman, a perplexed expression coming to his ghostly and unseen face. "Who the devil be you?" He came nearer. "And why do you look so very like my Aggie?"

Since Marie Aldworth could neither see nor hear her ghostly interlocutor, she could not reply to his perplexed query. She was awake to the presence of something alien in her bedchamber and she stared into the darkness, telling herself she was being foolish, that Delia's fears had encroached upon her own imagination. And still she could not get over the sensation of someone being near. Not precisely frightened, she was uneasy enough to come wide awake. She looked towards Delia, who slept soundly. Then she searched out the corners of her bedchamber in search of the reason for her unease.

The dawn found her dozing, her eyes closed but her senses still half-awake to the unfamiliar sounds of the ancient house.

4

THE NEXT DAYS passed quickly, Marie determined to have everything in readiness for her father's arrival. Lady Agatha, true to her word, helped the young newcomer staff the abbey and replenish its larders.

Margaret, June, and May were recommended by Fannie and accepted by Marie, sight unseen. Delia Dutton was of the opinion they should be interviewed first but Marie put her tiny foot down quite firmly. All three maids had worked for Lady Agatha, who now recommended them to Marie. There was no need of further references or questions.

Muttering to herself about the follies of impulsive youth, Delia disappeared to the upper regions of the house to supervise the storage of linens and inventory the household contents. She knew what she knew, Delia told herself, and what she did not know was how careful a housekeeper Lady Agatha was. Many titled ladies had no idea how much pilfering went on right under their upper-class noses.

Delia Dutton kept a sharp eye on the new maids, seeing to their work and making sure of their honesty. Lady Agatha took Marie on a tour of the large house, Marie noting what she would need to replace or refurbish. When her lists were made, Marie travelled with Fannie Burns to the village of Wooster to set up her accounts and see to the stocking of provisions and supplies. Young Tim drove the ancient abbey coach, fetching and carrying parcels and purchases for the better part of a week as Marie gathered everything she could think of in preparation for her father's arrival.

Whilst the abbey bustled with activity, Sir Harry kept to himself in the old nursery and the attics just above. Banished by the noise and busyness from the lower floors, the abbey ghost mulled over the conundrum of the young woman who looked so very like Agatha. The girl spoke Frenchy when she was alone with her abigail, which seemed highly

suspicious to the old campaigner who had lost his own life
aboard HMS *Victory* under Admiral Keppel.

The abigail was a sour-faced spinster who ordered the
maids about in stentorian tones more appropriate on the
battlefield than in the upper regions of Steadford Abbey.
All in all, Sir Harry the Ghost was positive something
havey-cavey was going on, but for the life, or death, of
him, he could not figure out what it could be or why
the Frenchified young Miss Marie was living at Steadford
Abbey.

He found out sooner than he expected when on the
following Wednesday an elegant equipage arrived under
the great stone archway at the bottom of the abbey hill.
Clip-clopping at a smart pace, a phaeton, spit-polished to
a lustrous black and drawn by a handsome pair of matched
greys, passed under the gate clock and pressed onwards.
Following the curving abbey road the phaeton ascended
towards the crest of the hill, driving through the long avenue
edged by copper beeches.

The abbey grounds were in full bloom, the summer afternoon heady with the scents of roses and tuberoses, mignon-
ette and heliotrope. At the top of the hill stood a castle three storeys high. Built of honey-coloured stones, it
glowed golden in the slanting rays of the late afternoon
sun, surrounded by lavender spokes of catmint and masses
of fragrant pink china roses.

A wide portico with wide, shallow stone steps led between
large oriel windows supported by sturdy stone corbels to a
huge iron-banded oak door. Young Tim came around the
far side of the house in time to see the stylish carriage
come to a halt at the abbey steps. Startled, he watched
the two tall, powerful-looking men who descended from
the phaeton.

"You, there," the shorter of the two men called to the
groom.

Tim recognised the voice of authority and doffed his cap,
coming at a run to brake in front of the stranger, beside the
matched greys. "Yes, sir?"

"I take it you work here?"

"Yes, sir. I'm Young Tim."

Will Carston stared down at Tim, bushy dark eyebrows beetling together. "*Young* Tim?"

"Yes, sir. It's what they've called me since I was a young one."

"Then it's time they stopped. I am Will Carston and I shall call you Timothy."

"Yes, sir." Tim cast a quick glance towards the taller man, who was leaning down to inspect the hind leg of the nearer grey.

"You may see to the luggage, Timothy, and then to the horses." Will Carston turned towards the man behind him, ignoring the awkward young man who outright stared at the new master of Steadford Abbey.

"Is he hurt?" Will asked, bending to look at the grey's hind leg.

"The wheels must have thrown up a sharp stone," was the reply. The man who made it had a deep voice which matched his powerful frame. Dark hair threaded with grey at the temples surrounded a face which bore the marks of sunburn and battle. Both his face and his dark eyes were hardened with what the world had shown him in his last half-century of life. "He's badly cut."

"He'll be needing a good cleaning and one of Homer's special poultices," Tim put in, forgetting his place. The tall man straightened up and turned piercing black eyes to meet Tim's own gaze. Tim blushed to the roots of his ginger hair. "It's Homer th-that takes care of all the cattle hereabout," Tim stammered.

Will Carston took pity on the boy. "Like as not he's never seen horseflesh such as this pair, Timothy."

"Oh, yes, he has," Tim blurted. "His grace had a pair of greys, prime goers they were too, and Homer did for them and never a complaint."

"Who are you?" the taller man asked bluntly.

"I'm Homer's apprentice," Tim replied, pride in his voice. "I've worked for the abbey and Lady Agatha since I was a lad of twelve."

"Lady Agatha does not own the abbey," the man said.

Young Tim bristled at the dismissive tone in the newcomer's voice. "That's as may be," he said, his voice rising as he continued. "And her dead brother may have done her out of her rightful inheritance and left her only the abbey gatehouse, but she's the last of the Steadfords and the only rightful owner of Steadford Abbey!"

"That's enough, lad," Will Carston said as Fannie Burns came out onto the colonnaded porch, followed by Lady Agatha.

Tim was facing the men. "And any as says she isn't the finest lady they've ever met has the whole of the county to reckon with and that's flat!" he said boldly, not seeing the two women until Marie Aldworth came through the door.

"Papa!" the young woman exclaimed, her face wreathed in smiles as she forgot all propriety and bounded down the steps and launched herself into her father's arms. "Oh, Papa, we're home at last!" she said as Tim cast a guilty look towards Lady Agatha.

High above their heads, at a small round attic window, Sir Harry the Ghost stared down at the small group on the gravel just beyond the wide portico.

"Lady Agatha," Marie called out, holding out her hand. "I am so glad you are here to see his homecoming, since you have helped so very much to ensure it would be a happy one. This, at long last, is my father, Major Daniel Aldworth. And his batman, William Carston," she added. "Papa, Will, this is Lady Agatha Steadford-Smyth, the former owner of the abbey, and her abigail, Miss Fannie Burns."

"One of the former owners," Lady Agatha corrected. She came forward, her polite smile fading as she met Major Aldworth's stern expression and cold eyes. She found herself unable to tear her gaze from the tall man's dark and brooding eyes. Will Carston was lost from her thoughts as her eyes met and held his employer's.

"The only owner as counts," Young Tim put in unrepentantly.

Lady Agatha did not hear Tim's words, but he earned a warm smile from Fannie Burns, even as she told the boy he'd best see to his chores. Marie was happily unaware of the undercurrents around her as she hugged her father and continued to speak. "Lady Agatha has been the most kind of neighbours, Papa, and has told me a great deal about our new home. You will want to know all its history, as it is quite remarkable and has been on this site for centuries! And she says there are other Aldworths in the county. Did you know we may have relatives nearby?"

"We have no relatives," Major Aldworth said, the words abrupt. He nodded brusquely to both Fannie and Lady Agatha, then turned his attention to Will Carston. "See to the grey," he said, ignoring Young Tim.

"Right, sir," Will replied.

"Lady Agatha," Marie began again, "you must delay your departure now that Papa is here and stay to tea. Isn't that right, Papa?"

Major Aldworth interrupted. "No," he replied ungraciously, earning a small startled sound from Fannie Burns and more than a little animosity from Young Tim. "Marie," her father continued, "I'm sure Lady Agatha has more pressing demands elsewhere. As for myself, I have been travelling for three days and two nights and want nothing more than a bath and a bed. I fear I should be at a loss for polite small talk."

Fannie bristled at the man's dismissive words. "I can well believe that," she said acerbically, earning a quick searching look from the major. The new owner watched the serving-woman deliberately turn her back on him. "Is there anything further you require before we leave, Lady Agatha?" Fannie asked, ignoring the large man whose handsome countenance belied a most unhandsome and disrespectful disposition.

"I'll just get the gig, then, shall I?" Tim asked.

"Timothy, you are to see to the luggage," Will reminded.

"Let him do as he pleases," the major told his batman. With a stiff military back the major gave the slightest of bows to the women. "If you will excuse me," he said and, before any could answer, he strode up the shallow steps and into the house.

"I'd best show him to his rooms," Marie said, rushing after the major and leaving Fannie and Agatha alone on the wide porch as Will Carston unhitched the greys from the spanking new phaeton and young Tim ran to fetch the gig.

"It's Lombard Street to a China orange that horrid man is going to make the most disagreeable of close neighbours," Fannie declared.

"Do not put yourself into a taking," Lady Agatha replied in a distracted fashion.

Fannie gave her employer a long and searching gaze, trying to read meaning into the furrowed lines of Agatha's forehead and the peculiar expression in her dark eyes.

"And why should I not?" Fannie asked, warming to her subject. "That great ox is nothing but an impertinent soldier with shockingly bad manners." She spoke loudly enough for his batman to hear as he reached for the horses' ribbons. "I'll warrant he'll find himself without a friend in the county if he don't learn proper respect when talking to his betters."

Will Carston kept his eyes to his chore and his opinions to himself as he turned the phaeton and headed down the abbey road towards the stables at the foot of the hill.

"Your ladyship?" Young Tim called. He stopped the ancient gig at the foot of the steps and leapt down to assist the ladies into the ancient carriage.

"Thank you," Agatha Steadford-Smyth replied in a small voice.

Her tone startled him. "Are you feeling poorly, your ladyship?"

She roused herself from her private thoughts and looked into Tim's guileless blue eyes. "I'm perfectly well, Timothy."

He gave a little nod towards the phaeton, which preceded them down the abbey drive, heading into the stables as Tim stopped at the gatehouse across the drive. "That Will Carston person says as how I should be called Timothy by all, as you always have done, your ladyship."

Fannie sniffed. "Issuing orders before they've even set foot inside the abbey."

"The man has the right of it," Agatha replied. "Timothy is a proper name for a grown man. Timothy is no longer a child."

Fannie pursed her lips and stiffened her back. "I'm sure I've never said he was." She sniffed again. "Mark my words, no good will come from that man owning your abbey."

"It is not my abbey," Lady Agatha pointed out.

Fannie gave her mistress a very speaking look. "The man," she pronounced, "is a complete boor."

As the gig headed towards the gatehouse, Marie accompanied her father across the entrance hall and towards the curving oak staircase. High above their heads a panelled ceiling of Spanish chestnut looked down past the Steadford family portraits that marched along the length of the Long Gallery towards father and daughter as they climbed the stairs towards the master's suite.

"Papa, you must be very tired indeed," Marie said in a troubled voice. "I assure you Lady Agatha is the most agreeable of neighbours and has been a great help to me since we arrived."

"Are you very cross with me?" Daniel Aldworth asked his daughter.

"I'm not cross, never cross. It is just that you did seem to be rather ungracious. I've never seen you so before."

They reached the first floor landing, Daniel reaching to tip his daughter's chin up and searching out the eyes that were so like his own except for their expression. Where his was wary, hers were innocent and kind.

"I promise I shall do the civil with the neighbours as soon as I've rested. Does that make you happy?"

Marie smiled wide, going on the tiptoe to kiss her father's wind-hardened cheek. "Having you here and having a home of our very own from which we never have to stir makes me very, very happy, Papa."

"Capital! Now show me where I can take off my mish and crawl between the sheets."

"Papa!" Marie remonstrated, but she still smiled. "I swear you have the manners of a Gypsy."

"Or a soldier?"

"Or a soldier," she agreed.

"Proper young misses do not swear," her father reminded her.

Delia Dutton came down the upper hallway, her stern features screwed up into an unnatural smile. "Major Aldworth, I had no idea you had arrived. Marie, did you assemble the staff?"

"Let's not go through all that drill," Daniel replied. "I haven't the stomach for it at present. Speaking of my stomach, I wouldn't mind a bit of bread and cheese and a pint of ale."

"Immediately," Delia replied. The abigail sped off upon her errand as Marie reached for the door to the master's suite sitting-room.

"Here you are, Papa." Marie opened the door and stepped inside. She glanced around to ensure all was as it should be and then looked expectantly at her father.

Daniel Aldworth checked just inside the doorway. The sitting-room was most obviously a masculine abode with capacious, sturdy chairs and dark-toned colours. Marie chattered about the abbey as her father just stared at the room before him.

Wainscotted with honey-coloured oak, the walls were covered with a dark blue paper flecked with tiny golden crescents. A horsehair settee covered in rich blue fabric stood between cherrywood tables, cherrywood chairs scattered about, an upholstered leather wing chair in front of the black marble fireplace.

"Papa?" Marie touched the sleeve of her father's uniform. "Papa?"

The faraway look left his dark eyes as he looked down into her concern. "What is it?" he asked.

"Are you quite, quite sure we shall not drown in the River Tick, trying to run this household?"

Daniel Aldworth grinned, his forbidding features suddenly sunny, giving a glimpse of the youth he had once been. "Are you afraid we shall be nabbled off to debtor's prison, my sweet?"

"Laugh as you like," she told him in what she hoped were stern tones, "but I never had in mind such a house as this when you said we should finally settle down at home."

"At home," Daniel repeated, drawing his little girl into his arms and hugging her tight. "For me, wherever you are is home, dear girl. But for you this can't seem much like home. Would you rather have settled in Brittany?"

"I feel quite at home in England, Papa, for you've talked of naught else since I was born."

"But you would be near your mother's family if we'd stayed abroad."

"Great aunts and uncles and cousins I've never met? Not a bit of it." She dismissed them with a wave of her hand. "You are my family and England is our home and I am excessively pleased with the abbey, even if I do fear it is much too large for the two of us. You are sure we can afford to set up so grand an establishment?"

"Very sure," her father replied. "It is well within the means of the legacy I received from Sir Henry. Now, does that make you feel better?" he asked, seeing the worry leave her face.

"Yes," she told him, smiling wide. "Very much better."

"Good. Now leave me in peace."

"But your tray—"

"Tell Delia to leave it here and go."

Marie kissed her father's cheek and then did as he bid, leaving him to the silence of the empty rooms as she went in search of her abigail.

Daniel stood where he was for a few long minutes. His gaze went to the open door to the bedchamber beyond. The same wainscotting, the same gold-flecked dark blue paper patterned walls of the inner room. He walked forward finally and crossed the room, glancing into the valet's small bedroom, into the smaller dressing room and richly appointed private bath, before stopping in front of the

west-facing windows. Beyond the wide grassy lawns, past
a stand of ancient oaks, the distant glimmer of the River
Stour reflected the afternoon sunshine back towards the
high clouds and soft blue sky.

The scene was beautiful and it hurt his heart. Daniel
Aldworth turned away from the windows, unbuttoning his
shirt absentmindedly, his tired brain shutting out all thoughts
of the future. Or the past.

In the topmost attics of the huge old house another
Aldworth paced in ghostly boots three feet off the attic
floor. His features a study in distraction, Sir Harry the
Ghost did not bother to think up schemes to frighten the
new owners away. The new owners were in worse danger than any ghost could devise and well Harry knew
it.

In his mind's eye he could see Ambrose Steadford as
he was almost half a century ago, cursing Harry and all
the Aldworths who ever were, cursing any Aldworth who
dared henceforth set foot inside Steadford Abbey. That evil
curse had helped send Harry to the limbo of ghostly existence where he had hovered ever since, halfway betwixt life
and afterlife.

Harry himself had sealed his own doom, berating the
heavens above, reviling the gods on high for allowing the
terrible turn of events that had parted him from his beloved.
All he wanted was to be close to his beloved Aggie; it was
all he had ever asked, would ever ask, he had railed. And
the gods had heard him. They answered his pleas with their
own peculiar logic, allowing him to be close to Agatha precisely as he asked. But even as they granted the letter of his
wish, they denied him the substance, condemning him to a
ghosthood in which Agatha, herself, could never know he
was near.

Sir Harry gave up his pacing. He dropped down upon an
aged brass-banded trunk, sunk deep in thought, ruminating
on the sorry state of his current existence. His tattered purple velvet coat blended into the darkening shadows as the
sun plummeted from sight, leaving the world bereft of
warmth.

* * *

Many hours later the abbey was filled with deep night shadows. Marie woke from a troubled slumber, blinking in the half-light from the fire smouldering in the grate across her bedroom. The faint sounds of slippered feet came from the hallway beyond her bedroom, an even fainter trail of candlelight edging under her door as the steps came closer. The light flickered past and out of sight as the sounds receded.

When the sounds and the light came back near her door, Marie sat up and reached for her night-robe and the candle that was guttering away on her bedside table. Delia deplored Marie's habit of falling asleep by candlelight, calling her charge to task for a lack of thrift, but the major had long since informed the serving-woman that his daughter could waste all the candles she pleased if the dark made her uneasy.

Taking the candle stub with her, Marie opened her door and peered out towards the stairwell. The house was sunk in midnight gloom, vast echoing silences and night draughts giving a feeling of brooding melancholy and a sense of imminent doom, as if some threat lurked in each of the dark corners and draught-filled halls.

The only nearby light, which came from her own small candle, pooled a soft yellow glow down across her feet and the carpeted floor directly ahead of her. Far ahead, in the Long Gallery that curved L-shaped around the wide stairwell, another candle flickered.

Marie squinted, trying to make out the features of the dark form who walked along the Long Gallery's row of portraits, flashing light out at one after another of the Steadford family portraits. She hesitated, then walked resolutely, if slowly, forward, castigating herself at every tardy step for being a timid goosecap. She was a soldier's daughter. She had enough brass to overcome her childish fears of the dark.

As she silently upbraided herself, she came close enough to see that it was her father pacing far ahead of her. Fear turned to concern as she came closer, watching as he stood

for long, long moments peering intently at one of the portraits at the far end of the gallery.

When she came alongside, she saw it was the portrait of
a pinched-faced man whose small dark eyes and drooping
side-whiskers gave him a most unfriendly appearance. A
small brass plate on the portrait's ornate frame gave the
subject's name in flowing script: Ambrose Steadford.

"Papa?" Marie whispered. Her father seemed not to hear
her. She took another step towards him as he moved, finally, pausing in front of Agatha Steadford's portrait, lost in
his own thoughts. "Papa?" she repeated.

He heard his daughter the second time, turning towards
her with a frown. "Why are you up, little one?"

Marie smiled and reached for her father's arm. "I heard
noises and worried that ghosties and goblins were sneaking
about in the halls."

"And you, who fear the dark even when you are safe
in your very own bed, you sallied forth to do battle with
ghosties and goblins?" Daniel quizzed his daughter. The
candlelit shadows outlined the sabre-cut scar that slashed
his left cheek.

"I don't fear the dark," Marie defended. "I simply do not
like it. And as for ghosts and such, I would as lief face them
straight on as have them attack me in my bed," she added,
with a saucy toss of the thick dark hair that flowed loose
to her shoulders. "If I believed in them, which I don't."

"Foolhardy young miss," her father pronounced.

"And do you believe in them, Papa?"

Daniel Aldworth sighed long and deep, his tiredness
showing through his strained smile. "There are a great
many things I do not understand, my girl. No. I do not
believe in ghosts, but neither can I prove they do not
exist."

"And you never ran from battle in the peninsula," Marie
reasoned.

"No, I did not. But I certainly did not seek out battles
that were not mine, you impudent young hoyden." As he
spoke his face relaxed into softer lines, a suggestion of a
smile hovering around his eyes and mouth.

"What were you seeking amongst these dusty old portraits?" his daughter asked.

Daniel Aldworth hesitated. "Nothing," he answered after a silence. "I was merely restless; I felt the need of a short constitutional before retiring for the night. Now, young miss, it is long past time for you to be abed."

"And you?"

"And I," he agreed. He reached for Marie's arm and saw her eyes go back to the portrait of the lovely young Agatha. Daniel's own eyes flickered back to the portrait and then away as he drew Marie back along the Long Gallery and towards her bedroom. "We shall both retire to our beds."

Marie let her father lead her to her door and see her inside her bedroom. She waited in her doorway as he walked back to the master's suite. He hesitated, looked back at her concerned young face, and then went inside.

Slowly, Marie closed her door. The fire in the grate had died away to embers, her candle was only an inch high in its stand. As she climbed into bed she could still see her father's pensive expression as he stared at the Steadford portraits. She shivered and pulled her blankets up to her chin, closing her eyes and drifting back into a troubled sleep.

5

MAJOR ALDWORTH'S FIRST weeks at the abbey were marked by their quietness. The household which had been turned topsy-turvy in anticipation of the new master's arrival settled into a subdued routine of chores and meals. Calling cards were sent 'round from Squire Lyme and his wife, Marie penning her regrets that she and her father could not yet respond to their kind invitations. The major kept to himself and the company of his former batman, who now acted as valet and general factotum, running errands and accompanying the major on his forays afield from his rooms and the abbey library.

Occasionally Marie accompanied them on their rounds as they began to learn about the estate and meet the abbey tenant farmers or look in upon the stables and Homer's work with the abbey cattle and the major's own matched greys. But more often Marie found herself at loose ends, listening to Delia's endless lectures upon all manner of subjects and wandering the abbey's echoing halls by herself.

Marie told herself quite firmly she was not unhappy, she had no reason to be unhappy. She had prayed for the day when her father would no longer be a soldier, no longer put his life in danger for king and country, and that day had finally come. Her father was safe, they had at last established the permanent home she had dreamt of and it was a magnificent home at that, palatial and steeped in history.

How could she be so ungrateful as to be unhappy, she chided herself, and she had no proper answer. Except that the fact of her father's retirement from military service was very much different from what she had imagined. In truth, she had never conjured any real notions of what their life would be beyond a roseate vision of a vine-covered cottage somewhere deep in an English dell.

This idyllic vision was fostered by her homesick father from years of romantic tales he had spun about his homeland, the beloved England she had never seen save for one visit at the age of twelve. Her father's duties had taken them to London for one sweltering summer and the city had seemed filled to overstuffing with people, more people than she had ever seen in her entire life, all jammed into the nation's capital.

She remembered London ever after as filled with the din of a million conversations shouted at the top of everyone's lungs, a confusion of people and carriages and horses and buildings reaching towards the sky. It was nothing like her vision of a bucolic England and it had changed very little when she again saw it on her way to Dorset and her new home at Steadford Abbey.

The Dorset countryside was undeniably green and beautiful but the abbey spinney was hardly a vine-covered dell, and the abbey itself was much more castle than cottage.

Even her father was not as she had imagined. He seemed cheerless, and more silent than she'd ever known him to be, as if melancholia had descended upon him for some unknown reason. So as the weeks passed by Marie buried herself in unnecessary tasks, ensuring her cupboards were the most organised in the entire county and her inventories the most detailed and her needlework the most intricate, and not one word of complaint escaped her lips.

But there were idle moments as she slipped into her bed at night when the hobgoblins of ennui and worry and loneliness attacked her peace of mind.

One morning in October Marie woke from troubled dreams, feeling a presence in her room. Her sleepy eyes opened to see a shimmering shape hovering betwixt her bed and the window.

"Wha—?" she said as she rose on her elbow, squinting into the morning light. She blinked and it was gone. But the hairs on the back of her neck were standing straight up, her body and mind coming wide awake.

She raced towards the window, seeking out a trace of the apparition that was gone as suddenly as it appeared. She searched the ledge beyond her window and the ancient oak beyond the ledge but she could find nothing to confirm her fleeting impression of an alien presence.

In the distance she caught sight of her father, already up and pacing down the abbey drive. Grabbing her night-robe, she flung it around her shoulders as she ran barefoot into the upstairs hall and down the stairs. She dashed out of doors, racing towards her father. She was out of breath when she neared the gatehouse rose garden and called out to him.

The major was passing the gatehouse when he heard his daughter call to him. He stopped and turned back to see Marie flying towards him in her nightclothes and bare feet, a robe flapping from her shoulders.

"What has happened?" he asked, his frown deepening as he listened to his daughter's explanation.

"Papa, there was something strange in my room and it woke me up but when I tried to find it, it was gone!" Her excited tones rose higher and higher.

"Lower your voice," her father said sternly. "Now what foolishness is this you are prattling on about?"

"I saw something!"

"What did you see?"

"I—well, I can't precisely say, that is I don't precisely know. But it was transparent! I think it might have been a ghost."

"Marie Aldworth, I'm ashamed of you," he replied sharply. Her expectant face fell into chagrined lines. "You are much too old to be racing about in such a manner. I warrant, you would put a hoyden to the blush."

"I'm sorry, Papa."

"Is there a problem?" Fannie Burns stood on the far side of the gatehouse garden wall, peering over the ancient stones towards father and daughter.

"None that need concern you, Miss Burns." Daniel was abrupt with Lady Agatha's abigail. He returned his attention to his daughter, pointedly ignoring the woman who scowled at him from behind the waist-high stone wall. "You are to return to your room this very instant and dress yourself in proper attire, young miss."

"But, Papa—the ghost—"

"But me no buts or I shall have Delia prepare one of her remedies."

"But, Papa, I'm not ill."

"You are either ill or demented to wander about in such attire and speaking nonsense."

"Yes, Papa," Marie said meekly as her father turned away. Cane in hand, he traversed the gravelled drive from gatehouse to stableyard and disappeared inside the abbey stables.

Marie saw Fannie still scowling over the wall. "I'm terribly sorry if I disturbed you, Miss Burns."

Fannie's expression softened as she answered the girl. "You've done naught to apologise for, Miss Marie. But I cannot say the same for that gruff and surly father of yours. Is he *always* in a bad temper?" she asked in exasperation.

"Oh, no, Miss Burns, I assure you, Papa has the most pleasant disposition."

"I've seen no sign of it."

Marie sighed. "It's true he's been most awfully gloomy of late. But this is not the least bit normal for him," she defended. "As a rule he is the most jolly and pleasant and understanding of men."

"Then he should stop hiding his light under such a large bushel," Fannie replied acerbically.

Marie only half-heard the older woman's comment. "I cannot understand why he should be so unhappy."

Fannie grimaced. "He's a man."

"I beg your pardon?"

"Men are drawn to adventure and danger as bees are drawn to honey. If there's no war going, they'll create one just to keep themselves occupied. You take a man like your father, used to commanding great hordes of soldiers and dashing into battles and whatnot and put him in a quiet backwater such as this and he doesn't know what to do with himself."

Marie's beautiful face paled, Fannie's words raising more doubts to trouble her thoughts and sink her deep into gloom.

"I cannot help but be uneasy at the thought that he should so dislike our new home."

"Mark my words, he'll soon make longer and longer journeys away and spend less and less time in the country."

"But where shall he go and what will he do?" Marie asked.

"He'll find gaming tables and willing enough light skirts, no doubt, for he's handsome to a fault but to me handsome is as handsome does."

"Oh, no!" Marie replied, shocked to the core. "I don't mean to correct you, but I assure you, Miss Burns, my father is nothing like that sort of gentleman. He would never stoop to such practices."

"You are very young and innocent, Miss Marie. *All* men are that sort. Mark my words, before winter is upon him he'll most likely have hied himself off to London gaming clubs and from there into all manner of peculiar masculine activities."

"He never shall," Marie defended. The thought of the strange vision that had awakened her intruded. "Miss Burns, the most peculiar thing happened this morning. I saw . . . something . . . in my bed chamber." Marie poured out her story, her excitement rising as she retold what had happened.

Fannie listened to the garbled report and then shook her head. "Miss Marie, it sounds to me as if Hetty Mapes has been busy filling your ears full of old nonsense about the abbey ghost."

"Then there is an abbey ghost?" Marie's eyes widened in awe. "Oh, do tell me every single particular."

"There's naught to tell. An old house has its own creaks and groans just as we do ourselves as we get on in years. You should pay no attention to Hetty Mapes and her fanciful tales. Suggestible girls have scared themselves and that's all that's ever happened and that's the truth of it."

"But I've not talked to Hetty nor she to me about any ghosts. Miss Fanny, I didn't hear creaks and groans, I saw it!"

"A trick of light," Fannie dismissed.

Marie considered the possibility. "Are you quite sure that was all it could be?" She sounded disappointed.

Hoofbeats approached as Fannie replied that she was most decidedly sure. Both women looked up at the handsome young man riding towards them. He reined in his bay and jumped to the ground, a pleasant smile lighting his eyes.

"Oh I do say, Fannie, what have you been hiding from me? A wood nymph from the depths of fair Camelot's forests?"

"I've hidden nothing and you, Master Hero, had best turn your head the other way," Fannie told the newcomer.

"I am your most obedient etcetera and I shall do exactly as you say but first you must introduce me to the fair damsel whom I sorely hope is in distress. I should very much enjoy rescuing such a one from whatever cruel fates have sent her forth in her petticoat."

"I am not in my petticoat," she defended. She drew her robe closer about her nightgown, fastening it as the handsome blond man smiled lazily at her. "And you needn't speak of me as if I were not present," she added saucily. "I do not enjoy it."

The gentleman bowed low. "I most abjectly apologise, dark beauty."

Marie felt uncomfortably warm suddenly, and more than a little self-conscious.

"Hero Hargrave," Fannie began, "you'd best learn to hold your tongue as Miss Aldworth's father is a military man and a major at that, besides being the abbey's new owner. He'll not take your jesting kindly, I can tell you that. He'd be in his rights to give you a proper melting. Miss Marie, if you know what's best for you, you'll do as your father bid and hie yourself home before he returns from the stables and finds you still in your nightwear and talking to strangers."

"Shocking," Hero replied, casting so roguish a look at the abigail that she almost burst out laughing. Fannie contained her amusement at great cost, her lips thinning into a repressive line as she attempted the sort of glance Lady Agatha would use to put a young person in his proper place.

Marie was already starting away when Hero caught up with her. "Miss Aldworth, allow me to escort you."

"Mr. Hargrave, we have not been formally introduced. I must go," Marie added.

"It wouldn't be proper," Fannie put in.

Hero glanced from Marie's unfettered hair, which cascaded down to her shoulders, to the thin wrapper she wore and the edges of the white cotton chemise beneath to her slim and naked feet. "Propriety is not a problem," Hero said with a winning smile. "I have never been the least bit proper, as all who know me can attest."

"Sir!" Marie remonstrated. "That is a sorry history, if true, and one of which you can hardly be proud."

"I did think you might not be such a high stickler yourself, Miss Aldworth." He drawled his words, a small smile curving the corners of his mouth.

Marie Aldworth blushed crimson to the roots of her hair. "I assure you," she said stiffly, "this is a most unusual occurrence."

"All the more reason I must come to the rescue," Hero proclaimed. And as Fannie watched he reached for Marie's waist. She gave a little shriek as she was flung up upon the saddle, Hero mounting behind her.

"Let that girl go!" Fannie demanded in shocked accents.

"Merely seeing Miss Aldworth to her door, no need to discompose yourself, Fannie. Please inform Lady Agatha I've received a letter from Andrew and I shall be back presently to deliver it for her to read."

The stallion reared up as Hero wheeled the bay around and headed up the abbey hill.

"And what of Charlotte Summerville?" Fannie called out as they started away.

"Tut, tut," he shouted back as he let the stallion have its head, "that's terribly old news. Besides, Charlotte's found herself a viscount!"

Fannie watched them race up the hill, Marie's long dark hair streaming out behind as Hero's blond head leaned over her, keeping her safely in his arms. Shaking her head,

Fannie turned back towards the gatehouse kitchen and her morning chores.

Inside the large warm kitchen Lady Agatha sat by the window, her sewing basket open beside her.

"Fannie?" Lady Agatha questioned her servant's preoccupied expression. "Did I see young Hero ride up?"

"He's gone to the abbey."

Lady Agatha was sorting out thread. "I was not aware the Hargraves were acquainted with the new owner."

"I don't know what the world is coming to," Fannie told her employer. "The men have no manners and the younger generation has no sense. It's all these foreign entanglements if you ask me."

"What?"

"Hero said he is bringing a letter from Andrew and Alice."

"Fannie Burns, you are not making any sense."

"That may be but if so, I'm in good company then," Fannie sniffed. "Hero will be here presently. He's taken the young Aldworth girl back to the abbey. And if you had seen the girl, or her dour father for that matter, you'd not be quizzing me about not making sense. Why should I make sense when all about are going mad?"

Having no reply to such a strange statement, Lady Agatha retreated into her work of sorting threads and needles.

At the top of the hill Marie slid off the bay and away from Hero's grasp. He watched her race up the wide, shallow steps.

"Good-bye, beautiful apparition," Hero called.

Marie hesitated at the front door and threw a glance back at the young man. She hoped it would be quelling but his grinning countenance showed no signs of remorse.

"Good-bye, sir," Marie said, her head held high. She opened the door and swept inside in as regal a fashion as she could muster but once inside her posture wilted at the sight of Delia Dutton.

"Miss Marie! I do not believe my eyes!"

Marie ran up the stairs towards her room, Delia following close behind, questioning her charge in scandalised accents.

6

FANNIE BURNS ARRIVED at the abbey the next afternoon and made herself comfortable in the kitchen over a cup of Hetty Mapes' scalding hot tea.

"I've brought a list of the things Lady Agatha needs from the market," Fannie told the abbey cook. "And she's sent along her receipt for the heating salve you asked about."

"My lumbago and I shall thank her this very evening, I can tell you that for a fact." Hetty Mapes was a large woman who had grown even larger and rounder over the years. She reached to rub her back and then, with a decidedly contented sigh, settled to a stool on the opposite side of the kitchen table from her guest. "Young Tim will be off at first light so as to be back in time to help the new master in the stables. He's quite caught up with our abbey horseflesh, Mr. Carston says."

Fannie made a derisive sound. "It's a wonder the major doesn't terrify the poor brutes."

"Fannie Burns, I've never heard you speak so uncharitably. And about the abbey's new owner, at that. Why, you hardly know the man."

"I know his bad-tempered ill manners have put me out of all charity."

"He's a quiet sort," Hetty said, defending her new master. "And an officer, not to mention he's as handsome as they come."

"Handsome is as handsome does," Fannie replied. "And if you ask me, any man who snubs Lady Agatha is beneath contempt."

Hetty's eyes grew as round as her face. "He snubbed Lady Agatha?"

"He was rude when he arrived and he's not called on her since, nor even sent his card."

Hetty Mapes shook her head. "I can hardly credit it," she responded.

"And have you heard the way he speaks to his daughter?" Fannie asked.

"No, I've not," Hetty admitted.

"Well, then, you can hardly judge, now can you?"

"I've barely seen the new master, truth be told, although I've spoken a few times to his man, Will Carston. And a right agreeable gentleman's gentleman that one is, I can tell you. The best I've ever seen and one you might set your cap for, Fannie Burns."

Fannie was so startled she nearly spilt her tea. "Set my cap for!" she responded in scandalised tones.

"I have the greatest respect for your opinion," Hetty continued placidly. "But I cannot think that Will Carston would serve an unprincipled master."

"It would seem Mr. Carston has made a most favourable impression on you. But that doesn't change the facts." As Fannie spoke Hetty glanced towards the hallway. The abbey's new owner stopped in the doorway as Fannie continued.

"Major Aldworth may or may not be principled, I've no idea," Fannie told the abbey cook in sharp accents.

"Fannie, you don't mean that," the abbey cook said desperately, casting speaking glances at Lady Agatha's servant.

"I most assuredly do. He is a most disagreeable brute and far too high-handed if any should ask me."

A male voice replied in frozen accents. "I am not aware that any have, Miss Burns."

Fannie turned around to see Major Aldworth scowling at her from the doorway. With one swift glance backwards at Hetty, Fannie faced her questioner squarely. "It's still a free country and I've a right to my opinions," she told the man unrepentantly.

The major's scowl deepened. "If you will please follow me—" He spoke in a cold voice that brooked no objections.

Fannie thought about defying him, but he was already

walking away. "You see what I mean?" she said to Hetty under her breath.

Hetty Mapes watched with worried eyes as Fannie followed Major Aldworth towards the green baize door far down the servants' hall.

Major Aldworth himself, with barely controlled anger, stalked through the green baize door, letting it slam back towards his follower. Expecting nothing better from the uncouth man, Fannie's arm was outstretched, her hand stopping the door's swing and sending it open again, charging through it with determined steps.

She was hard put to keep up as he paced the length of the west hall towards and into his book-lined study. The room was smaller than the library; the bound and unbound folios on the study bookshelves were the written records of the abbey itself. Almost four hundred years of household accounts, tenant accounts, inventories and family bibles. The oldest parchment scrolls were in Latin, records of the ancient abbey's original monks.

The first Steadford records were sketchy, the family almost wiped out in Bloody Mary's reign but finally in the stability of Good Queen Bess's long reign the secret doors were forgotten, no longer needed to protect the abbey's occupants from its sovereign's murderous whims.

Some of the names on the current tenant farmer roles went back to the earliest abbey records; all of them had family names that cropped up, fathers, sons and grandsons, from one century to the next.

Lady Agatha's serving-woman watched the new owner settle himself behind the massive carved desk that had belonged to Lady Agatha's father's grandfather. The man paid no attention to the woman who stopped in front of the desk and waited. She watched him open an account book from a pile that lay on his desk and still he did not look up.

Fannie's patience snapped in the long silent moments when he seemed to deliberately ignore her presence.

"You asked me to follow," she reminded him in cutting accents.

Daniel Aldworth looked up at the woman with a scowl that had once sent his officers scurrying out of his tent to do as he said. His dark eyes met Fannie's clear blue ones and neither gave the other any quarter.

When he could not best her with his scowl he spoke in words that froze as they hit the air between them. "You are a servant, are you not?"

"I am Lady Agatha's abigail," Fannie replied proudly. "Not *your* servant."

Daniel's eyes betrayed a flicker of surprise at her audacity. She was either appallingly presumptuous or very sure of herself, the major decided.

"Nevertheless, I assume you have some small knowledge of the abbey's accountings and books."

"I have much more than some, Major Aldworth. I have posted Lady Agatha's books for these thirty years past."

The handsome man slowly raised his brow, irritating Fannie further. "Good" was all he said.

"I beg your pardon?" Fannie said in her most repressive manner.

The major seemed not to notice her words. "I intend to put the abbey accounts in order."

Fannie gave him an arch look. "A worthy intention," she replied caustically.

He swept his arm wide to include all the bound volumes around them. "Prior to 1804 all is in order but the current records are very spotty, especially the tenant farmer accounts."

"Prior to 1804 Lady Agatha owned the abbey and I kept the books." There was pride in Fannie's voice.

"So I was told," Daniel replied dryly. "Is it possible, if Lady Agatha has no objections, for you to help me verify the accuracy of the current accounts?"

Fannie's surprise showed. "I very much doubt it," she replied after a moment of confusion.

Daniel Aldworth stood up. He came around the massive desk, towering over the serving-woman, his brow knitted together into scowling lines. "I will, of course, pay for your time. I am not asking that you like me, Miss Burns. Merely that you assist in rectifying the abbey records. Surely Lady Agatha would wish the tradition of hundreds of years continued."

"I shall ask Lady Agatha," Fannie replied in a noncommittal tone.

"Good. I'd like to start as soon as possible."

Fannie bridled. "I did not say I would do it."

Daniel's dark eyes narrowed as he studied the woman before him. Of a good height for a woman and nicely rounded in all the right places, Fannie had intelligent blue eyes set in a pleasing face. Her fifty-three years sat easily upon her, the fine lines around her eyes belying a tendency to smiles that Daniel himself had yet to see.

Uncomfortable under the man's penetrating gaze, Fannie spoke with more force. "Nor did I say Lady Agatha would permit me to work with you."

"I very much doubt anyone or anything could stand in your way if you wanted to do something."

Fannie thought she heard a grudging compliment in the man's words. She watched him carefully.

"What is your full name?" Daniel asked.

Fannie was taken aback. "What?"

"What is your name?"

"Why?" she asked suspiciously.

"Fannie is sometimes short for Frances."

"Not in my case. Fannie Rose Burns I was christened."

The abbey's new owner turned away. "I shall await your decision."

"And if I say no?"

Daniel hesitated. "I shall be disappointed," he said ambiguously. But he did not turn back to face her. After a few silent moments he heard the door open and close behind him.

A very distracted Fannie Burns left the new owner and headed through the abbey's empty halls towards the outer door. Distant kitchen sounds, muffled by the walls and doors between, echoed softly in her wake. Fannie thought about going back to bid Hetty good-bye but, in the end, she wanted to escape from Daniel Aldworth more than she wanted conversation with the abbey cook.

The air was autumnal crisp outside as Fannie walked down the abbey hill. The slanting rays of afternoon sunlight dappled the drive and the honey-coloured rough-hewn stones of the gatehouse at the end.

On her way, Fannie went over and over the recent conversation with Major Aldworth. He was such a strange and moody man, definitely not easy to know. She thought about his questioning her name, a bemused expression on her face. What could have made him curious about a thing like that, she asked herself, and had no answer.

If she was a tiny bit less irritated with the major than she had been before their talk, she was not about to admit it. He was gruff, insensitive and mannerless, as she had told Lady Agatha that very morning. And his asking after her name made him no less rude.

Letty Merriweather was ensconced in the gatehouse parlour with Lady Agatha when Fannie arrived back. Fannie took one swift look at her mistress's face and left to fetch biscuits and tea.

"I am surprised to see you again so soon after your last visit," Lady Agatha was saying with the most polite accents she could muster.

"Oh, I do hope I am not usually remiss in my duties, Lady Agatha. Not that I think visiting *you* is a duty," Letty said virtuously. "But I know how sedentary you are these days and how you must pine for news of all the county comings and goings."

"I've never pined in my life," Agatha responded sharply, nettled at the widow's description. She could well imagine Letty Merriweather busily wagging her tongue all over the countryside about *poor* Lady Agatha, sedentary and failing in her elder years. "I'm as fit as you, yourself, Leticia Merriweather and I've never felt better in my life."

The twinge she felt in her shoulder when she moved her hand for emphasis she ignored, along with the sciatica that stabbed within her hips when she sat too long in one position.

A low murmur of voices came from the kitchen. Agatha
called out to Fannie, who appeared in the kitchen doorway,
Marie Aldworth just behind.

"I didn't mean to disturb you and your guest, Lady
Agatha," the girl began but Lady Agatha smiled at her.

"Nonsense, I'm most glad you've come." Lady Agatha
spoke with more vehemence than she realised but her meaning was lost on Letty as the little widow smiled up at Marie
Aldworth.

"We've not been introduced," Letty put in. "I'm Leticia
Merriweather."

Lady Agatha spoke slowly. "This is Miss Marie
Aldworth."

"Aldworth?" Letty repeated the last name, glancing from
the girl to Lady Agatha and giving the dowager a very
speaking look. "It has been many years since we've heard
that name in Wooster."

Unaware of Lady Agatha's history, Marie answered the
widow. "I'm told there are other Aldworths who live in
Dorset."

"There used to be," Letty replied. She looked as if she
were about to say more but Fannie did not give her the
chance. To forestall the widow waxing eloquent upon the
subject of the Aldworths' and Steadfords' ancient quarrels,
Fannie said the first thing that came to mind.

"Miss Marie was asking about the young gentleman."

"Miss Burns!" Marie blushed scarlet, thrown into confusion by Fannie's bald words.

Lady Agatha frowned at her serving-woman but Leticia
Merriweather saw her opportunity and used it. "What young
gentleman? Perhaps I can be of some small help since I
know absolutely everyone in the county."

"I don't believe in wasting time with gossip," Agatha told
the round little widow.

"Oh, Lady Agatha," Marie said with real distress. "I hope
you do not think me a gossip."

"Not you, child."

"There was a gentleman you were asking after, Miss
Aldworth?" Letty could not contain her curiosity.

"No. That is, well, yes, but I was merely curious as to his name since he was so generous with his time."

"Leticia, she is merely speaking of young Hieronymus Hargrave, who came to visit me when Miss Aldworth was here," Agatha said in repressive tones.

"Ah, young Hero." Letty smiled up at Marie. "Such a handsome young gentleman, is he not? Why, I've known him since he was born—a very good family, the Hargraves. Young Hero is said to have led a rackety sort of life in London, all the social whirl and gaming with his friends in disreputable clubs. But he is still the pet of the Marriage Mart even though he's cried off from making any *permanent* liaisons."

Lady Agatha watched as Marie sat down beside Letty. Marie's eyes were alight with curiosity. "You make him sound quite the rake."

"He's a proper young man to his parents, mind." Letty gave Marie a prompting smile. "Your father is an army man, I understand?"

"Yes, a major."

"Ah, and you and your mother have been much separated from him, I daresay."

A shadow crossed Marie's dark eyes. "My mother and father were never apart. And I continued to travel with my father after my mother's death."

"I'm so sorry, I had no idea," Letty replied. "But then you've lived on the continent. Was your mother an English lady?"

"Leticia," Agatha said repressively but Marie was already answering.

"My mother was Belgian."

"Ah, then your father was with his grace of Wellington."

"He was seconded to the duke's staff during the treaty arrangements, yes."

"Then he might have made the acquaintance of our new squire, Captain Tompkins. Captain Thomas Tompkins."

"Leticia," Agatha said, "the army is very large. I very much doubt that they would have served together."

"I do seem to remember," Marie said, "that my father

knew a Captain Tompkins many years ago when I was small."

"Tompkins is a common enough name," Fannie put in as she brought in the tea.

"You will most certainly meet the captain at church. You are Church of England, are you not?"

"Yes, of course."

"Good." Letty patted the girl's hand. "One never knows what can happen to good English stock when they're forced to tarry too long on foreign soil."

With this bit of wisdom imparted, Leticia reached for a tea-cake and smiled up at Fannie, who was handing Lady Agatha a cup.

"Perhaps," Leticia said as Lady Agatha poured the tea, "you and your father will join me on Sunday. I would be most glad to introduce you around, as it were."

"I'm sorry, but my father is not in the habit of going to church."

Fannie gave an audible sniff at this latest news of Major Aldworth's shortcomings.

"I'm sure Lady Agatha and Fannie would be glad of your company," Leticia said. She smiled sweetly as Agatha handed her a cup of fresh-brewed tea. "We've missed them both these past few weeks and are quite, quite, at a loss without our Lady Agatha in attendance at our poor little services. And you, of course, Fannie."

Fannie grimaced but it was Lady Agatha who replied. "I very much doubt the Reverend Whipple would appreciate your use of those adjectives, Leticia. Sugar?" she continued as she filled a cup with tea for young Marie.

"Thank you, yes."

"When you and your father are settled in at the abbey we shall all look forward to your joining our small social circle," Letty chattered on, keeping up a steady stream of inconsequential small talk.

Marie answered all of Leticia's questions, giving the little widow the most enjoyment she had had in many a month as she stored up the information which she would soon be repeating to any who would listen. Agatha listened with only half an ear to the chatter around her as she settled back in her chair to sip her tea. She glanced out the window, losing the conversation around her as her thoughts went back to times long past.

7

THE FOOTMAN SENT to fetch her found young Lady Agatha in the kitchen with the cook.

"The master wants to see you," he said.

Agatha's good spirits drooped as she nodded and followed the footman out, leaving the warmth of the kitchen. The cook shook her head as she turned back to her work.

"It's a pity her mother had to die so young, leaving her to fend for herself."

"I'd trade places straight off, I would," the scullery maid replied.

"Trade places with Lady Agatha?" The cook gave an inelegant snort, her bony face widening with an ironic smile. "And have Ambrose Steadford for your father? Not I, my girl. Nor would I have that young Nigel as my brother, he who is so malicious and mean to the poor motherless child."

While the cook worried about her young mistress, Agatha herself was approaching her father's study with dragging steps. As she drew near she could hear the raised voices inside the closed door and hesitated with her hand on the knob.

"Nonsense, man," her father's deep voice resounded through the closed door and then another man answered him, not her brother.

She could not make out the other man's words, only the low murmur of his voice and her father's louder replies.

"She'll be most amenable, most amenable," Ambrose Steadford assured his listener. "Nigel, go see where your sister is!"

Agatha heard the sound of approaching footsteps and knocked lightly, opening the door just as Nigel reached it. Her brother was only a few years older than she, but he already had the pinched look and drooping mustache he would carry for the rest of his life. He was only an inch or two taller than his sister, a fact that gave him no end of irritation, and his subsequent querulousness was often attributed to his father's fixation on height and girth as a measure of a man's strength.

"There you are, at last," Nigel said. "You've kept father and his guest waiting."

Agatha knew perfectly well that the visitor was her brother's friend not her father's guest but she kept her peace and walked forward, dropping a respectful little curtsey. "Papa?"

"Where were you, girl?"

"I was helping Cook, Papa."

"There's no reason for you to hang about the kitchens. You're not going to be a cook, young miss. You're going to marry gentry."

Agatha saw her brother's friend watching her and blushed crimson to the roots of her dark chestnut hair. "Papa," she protested, but her father only laughed and nudged the guest's shoulder.

"She's a good girl, as you can see. Agatha, you remember Homer Smyth."

"Mr. Smyth," Agatha said politely, dropping a half-curtsey.

Homer Smyth raised his quizzing glass to one bored-looking pale blue eye. At thirty-one, he already showed the first signs of dissipation, his skin sallow and as pale as his thinning hair, his disposition coloured by too much wine and too many late nights.

Agatha averted her eyes from his ungallant stare. It was rude to be so blatantly curious and yet her father did not reprimand the man.

Homer Smyth's coat and waistcoat were of fairly conservative cut, with long buttonholes and coatsleeves with round cuffs falling away from the arm and his wig was a plain pigeon-winged toupee. But the colours he wore, from his flame-coloured coat to his yellow and green embroidered waistcoat, suggested a man who sought to be a London dandy. Fobs, seals and embroidered, scented handkerchiefs adorned his person, giving the pale man the look of someone whose clothes wore him.

"Yes, she'll do quite nicely," Smyth said with minimal tact.

Agatha looked from Homer Smyth to her father and thence to her brother Nigel, whose scheming little smile caused fear to rise within her breast. The man's strange words and her father's calm acceptance of them worried her even more than her brother's glee.

"Father?"

Ambrose Steadford studied his beautiful young daughter's concerned face. "You are to be married, girl, you should be delighted."

"Married?" She whispered the word as if it were a death sentence, her eyes going, in horror, to Homer Smyth's jaded expression. She went to her father's side, reaching for his arm. "Father?"

Her father scowled at her. "Smile or you'll heap disgrace upon your family."

"How can I smile?" she asked in a piteous tone that did nothing to assuage her father's contempt. "Father, you cannot ask this of me, you know that I already—"

"Silence!" he bellowed. "How *dare* you disgrace me in front of my guest?"

Agatha picked up her skirts and raced from the room, the sound of her father shouting after her loud in her ears as she ran down the abbey halls and up the stairs to the safety of her own rooms.

Once there, she threw herself on her bed, tears streaming down her cheeks. A sound behind her alerted her to Nigel's presence before he spoke.

"Father says you are to march right back down and apologise."

She sat up, rubbing at her eyes. She reached to replace the pins that had fallen from her thick dark curls in her headlong flight. "I shall do neither," she informed her brother.

"You will do both," he corrected softly. "You have no choice."

"You needn't gloat, Nigel, for I shall never marry that odious fool you call a friend. Papa himself has said Homer Smyth has no address and less fortune. I don't know how you persuaded Papa to this horrid course but you can rest assured you shall never get your way."

"I didn't persuade him, sister dear. You did."

"I!" Agatha's shock brought her to her feet. "How dare you say such a lie? I detest the man."

"Nevertheless, it is so," Nigel replied smugly. He watched her blanch as he spoke his next words. "You see, dear sister, you have been followed."

"I—I don't know what you mean," she said quickly, but there was a guilty edge to her voice and her eyes avoided meeting his.

"You know exactly what I mean."

Her brother's smug triumph infuriated her. "You've followed me yourself," she accused. "You are a mean-spirited and wicked man and I hate you!" Agatha tried to push past her smiling brother.

"Cook can't hide you this time, Agatha. You've been much too cosseted since Mama died." He stood in her doorway, blocking her escape. "Homer will teach you better manners!"

"Let me go," she insisted.

Ambrose Steadford's heavy-booted stride heralded his approach, his face bunched up into angry lines. "I ought to box your ears," he thundered.

"Papa, you can't want me to marry such a one as that," Agatha said with heart-rending feeling and then she shuddered. "When Nigel brought him last, you said yourself he was nothing but a tallow-faced twiddle-poop."

"That was then and this is now, girl, and I won't have my own chit making me look the buffle-headed clunch! I told him he had your hand and have it he does." Ambrose Steadford glowered at his daughter.

"I shall run away!" the young Agatha said dramatically.

"Think you'll run to that miserable greenhead wretch of an Aldworth, do you? Well, I shall show you what's what, my girl. I shall lock you in your room until you're well and truly wed!"

Agatha fell to her knees in front of her father. She reached for his hand, tears streaming down her cheeks as she beseeched him to disavow his judgement.

"I'll do anything you ask, anything, for ever and ever if you will only not ask me to marry such a one as that. I will live out my life seeing to your every need if you will only not ask me to marry Homer Smyth!"

Ambrose Steadford was not a man who readily changed his mind. Nor was he, he liked to think, an unfeeling man. He loved his daughter as much for her sweet nature as for her beauty, and so he hesitated. Truth be told, Homer Smyth was not a man of his own stamp, any more than his son Nigel was.

Nigel spoke to his sister, his voice insinuating itself into his father's thoughts. "For such a young miss and, I had thought, a sheltered girl living quietly here in the country, you sound quite the jade, sister Agatha. I shudder to think poor Homer shall find you have more knowledge of the other gender than a proper young miss ought. No doubt he'll have to teach you more pleasing ways."

"Nigel, how can you speak so?" His young sister wailed the words.

"He's got the right of it," Ambrose interrupted. "By God, I'll not allow such goings-on in my household!"

"What goings-on?" Agatha cried. "What undeserved calumny are you allowing Nigel to heap upon me?"

"Sister, why would I wish you harm?" Nigel asked innocently.

"Enough," Ambrose bellowed. He glared at his son, giving his daughter some little hope. "I've heard enough!"

"Papa—" Agatha began, only to be cut off in midsentence by that self-same gentleman.

"Enough," he repeated in even louder accents. "You have been foolish beyond permission because I have been too lenient."

"Yes," Nigel put in.

"Keep shut!" his father hollered, quelling his slender son before he returned his harsh gaze to his daughter's face. "You will marry and you shall never see that Aldworth pup again as long as you both shall live!"

"But Papa, why?" Agatha cried.

"Why?" her father roared. "He is an *Aldworth* and well you know it. His father is the underhanded coxcomb who stole my land and I shall never forget or forgive!"

"But we have more than enough land!" Agatha protested.

Her father's face reddened with anger. "You are an ungrateful, unnatural child! Nigel!"

Nigel moved quickly to follow his father, pushing Agatha back inside the room and twisting the huge iron key in its lock, locking her within her room.

"Papa!" Her cries went through the thick oak door. "Come back oh please, please, come back." She rattled the door, trying to open it, her sobs growing louder as the footsteps outside receded down the hall.

She could hear Nigel's wheedling but could not make out his words. What she did hear was her father's reply.

"Keep shut, you ninnyhammer, or I shall chuck the both of you out of my house!"

Agatha drooped against her locked bedroom door, hoping her father meant Nigel and his friend. Her father could not truly mean to enslave her to a husband not of her choosing, she tried to tell herself, but even as she tried she thought of all the women in all the world who had been so enslaved. Men had all the rights and they used them with ill grace and less compassion.

Except Harry.

Her heart raced at the thought of the tall and handsome Harry. He would save her if he knew her plight. He would make all come out right and in the end even her father would come around, that was her fondest hope.

But he could do nothing if he did not know! She straightened, her brain working double-quick. She had to get to Harry, to tell him, to warn him and to flee before her father had her bound for life to the odious Homer Smyth.

Nigel was determined she would wed his friend, why she did not know. But she knew Nigel thought of none but himself and never had. Her nurse had said long ago that her brother was a strange boy, and not her brother at all. Nigel was truly her cousin, her dead uncle's son, and raised as her father's heir since his parents' early death.

Perhaps a feeling of insecurity lent fuel to his envy and his greed, as if he must quarrel and defeat all others who had claim to his adopted father's affections. Perhaps, if Agatha's mother had survived, Nigel would have been less unfeeling, more generous. But his father, his mother and his adopted mother died while he was still very young and he clung to his adopted father in the only ways he knew how. Devious ways that undercut the other supplicant to Ambrose Steadford's heart and wealth.

She had to reach Harry, of that Agatha was very sure. She looked towards her windows and then ran to her wardrobe, changing to sturdy half-boots and fastening a long woollen cloak around her shoulders. Her windows looked out across the abbey grounds towards the hillsides far beyond the abbey hill. There was a ledge two feet beneath her windowsill. It ran the length of the house and around the back and west side beyond, the stone outcropping barely more than a foot wide.

Agatha unlatched her window, leaning out into the early evening breeze. In the twilight haze the ledge looked very narrow indeed. Summoning her courage she pulled a chair to the window and stepped up and, gingerly, out, one foot reaching down to touch the stone ledge. A little more sure of her purchase, Agatha shifted her weight to the foot on the ledge and pulled her skirts up, bringing her other foot outside as she grabbed the windowsill tightly and closed her eyes, breathing deep.

She stood stock-still for long moments, taking deep breaths. The evening breezes seemed stronger as she slipped one foot in front of the other, hugging the abbey's rough stones and closing her eyes. She edged towards the back of the abbey, moving inch by careful inch.

The corner where the east wall met the back of the abbey was adorned with an ornately carved column. The ledge ended on one side and began on the other. Forced to open her eyes, Agatha stared at the carved column only inches from her nose. The river winds whipped around the side of the building, reddening her cheeks and tugging at the long hairpins that kept her thick dark hair piled atop her head.

She almost gave up, only the thought of Homer Smyth propelling her forward. Her father would force her to marry the odious toad, Nigel would see to it. This very minute they were downstairs, sealing her doom. Her resolve stiffened by the realisation that she had no way to deter her father, short of running away, Agatha tried to calm her racing heart. Resolutely, and with bated breath, she reached around the thick column, offering up a fervent prayer as she moved. Her hand scrabbled for purchase on the other side, feeling blindly for any knob of plaster or outcropping stone she could grab onto. She clasped a piece of cold stone and, wrapping her fingers around it, she reached her leg around the corner, her skirts swirling out as her foot reached for and slipped off the edge of the stone outcropping. Startled, she gasped, her hands grabbing tight to the abbey stones as her foot slid farther onto the stone ledge beyond the pillar.

Right foot and hand committed to the back side of the ledge, left foot and hand still holding on the bulk of her weight on the east ledge, Agatha took one single deep breath and hopped forward, placing her weight on her right foot and holding on for dear life with her right hand.

She made it, her cheek pressed against the back wall, her breath erratic as she stood stock-still, calming her racing heart. Then, reminding herself her father or Nigel could go to her chambers at any moment, she edged her way forward as fast as she could go to the next turning, where another ornate column separated the back of the huge house from the west wall.

With quicker movements, Agatha reached her right hand out for purchase on the other side, grabbing a piece of stone and thrusting her right foot around the thick stone column, hurrying towards her destination. She moved too quickly, her right foot secure but her right hand grabbing a loosened piece of stone that came off as she put her weight on it. She stumbled, grabbing for another handful of stone and rock as she lost her balance and began to fall.

The dislodged rock flew past her shoulder, a shower of small pieces of stone flying by behind. Agatha grabbed at the unseen rock on the other side, scraping her knuckles as she fought to keep her feet on the ledge. She slipped to a crouching position as her fingers fought for and finally found a niche on the far side of the column. She hung on, gasping for breath as she looked down at the terrace far below.

By sheer willpower she pulled herself, slowly, up to a standing position. Shaking from fear, her teeth chattering from the cold winds and her own fright, she reached around the column and twisted herself across it to the ledge that ran along the west wall. Holding her breath, she made the last distance to her father's bedchamber windows and pushed on the first one. It wouldn't move.

She fought it and then reached for the second window and pushed harder. The window swung open and she climbed inside and jumped to the floor near her father's massive carved mahogany bed.

Agatha ran forward to the huge built-in clothespress and stepped into the wardrobe side that held her father's clothes on pegs. Shoving the clothing aside, she reached for the back wall and pressed against it. When the back slid aside, revealing a dark, dank chamber, she pulled the clothespress door shut behind her. She stepped onto the narrow stone staircase that spiraled downwards into utter blackness and raced down, heading for the ancient hidden priests' door.

She had to reach Harry before her father caught her.

- 8 -

LADY AGATHA ALLOWED Fannie to persuade her to accompany Marie Aldworth to the village church on Sunday but she was not prepared for Hero Hargrave's unheralded arrival that very morning. Sensing connivance on Fannie's part, Agatha gave her abigail a long and searching look as they sallied forth into the crisp October morning.

The early sun's rays bathed the eastern side of the abbey, warming the honey-coloured stones. Agatha looked up towards the ancient stone house, her eyes seeking out her own childhood window from amongst the windows that gleamed in the sun.

"Lady Agatha?"

"I beg your pardon?" She turned to face young Mr. Hargrave.

Hero's smile was the least bit tentative. "I was saying I hope you will accept my offer."

"I wasn't aware I was the one you were in search of this morning," Agatha told him, watching him falter a little before he had the grace to give her another lopsided smile.

"Am I so entirely transparent?" he asked.

"Youth often is," she replied. "Fannie?"

"Yes, your ladyship?"

"My, and aren't we formal this morning. If you think to earn your way back into my good graces, you are sadly off. I am vexed to the core with you and your meddling."

"I never did!" Fannie replied indignantly.

"You never stop," Agatha retorted.

Hero looked from Lady Agatha to Fannie. "Are you by any chance discussing me?"

"No," Fannie said.

"Yes," Agatha replied.

Left with this ambiguous information, Hero took the wisest course and kept his thoughts to himself. "Shall we?"

he asked, offering his arm to Lady Agatha who took it and allowed him to assist her up into his gleaming carriage. Hero settled Lady Agatha within the coach, then he turned to give Fannie his arm and winked.

"Aren't you forgetting someone?" she asked in an undertone.

"Absolutely not," Hero replied as she climbed into the carriage and called to his driver to carry on up the abbey hill.

At the abbey, Marie and Delia were just coming across the portico towards the drive, Delia continuing to complain about the distance to the village, when Marie spied the approaching coach.

"You see, you do not need to walk to the village," Marie told her servant. "Lady Agatha has seen to a coach."

" . . . worry a person to death," Delia ended under her breath. She placed a polite smile upon her face which soon turned to a frown when the coach stopped and a young man stepped out.

"Miss Aldworth." Hero swept a deep bow and then smiled wide, including Delia Dutton in his happy glance as he straightened. "It is a pleasure to escort you and your abigail to church."

"Mr. Hargrave," Marie replied primly, "how nice to see you again."

"Miss Marie," Delia said frowning, "I was not aware you had been introduced to any gentlemen since we arrived."

"We met at Lady Agatha's," Marie responded. Before Hero could say more she gave him a most repressive look and swept past him to the carriage.

"Lady Agatha, how kind of you to come and collect us," Marie said as Hero handed her inside. "Miss Burns, you remember Delia Dutton, I'm sure."

"Miss Dutton," Fannie acknowledged with a nod.

Delia gave a perfunctory reply, her attention upon the young man who climbed in last and sat across from her young charge.

Fannie saw the direction of Delia's gaze and tried to deflect it with words. "I hope all is well at the abbey."

"Yes," Hero chimed in. "We want to ensure you are so content with your new home that you needn't even think of your former life or pine for seasons in London or voyages away."

"We?" Delia interjected.

Hero did not seem to hear the servant's question, his eyes and ears so intent upon her mistress.

Marie dimpled as she smiled. "I can hardly think the county would miss us, as we are so new to the abbey and have yet to properly meet our neighbours."

"The abbey owners are always well known for miles around, Miss Aldworth," Hero said. "And one as fair as you will be the most popular of all. Since Lady Agatha, of course," he added hastily, glancing towards the lady in question. Because she was gazing out at the passing countryside, seemingly lost in her own thoughts, he returned his entire attention to the young beauty across from him on the upholstered benches. The carriage was high-sprung, swaying a bit more than lesser carriages but giving a very smooth ride down the rutted country roads.

Marie smoothed the skirt of her lemon-sprigged white muslin plain gown, the jonquil ribbons that edged her puffed sleeves fluttering. When she bent her head her face was shadowed by the white bonnet which was tied with yellow ribbons that matched her gown. Burnished dark mahogany locks peeked out from beneath the bonnet, curly strands edging her face. She looked up to see his infatuated gaze and gave him a saucy little smile.

"Was there something you wished to say, Mr. Hargrave?" she asked teasingly.

"Oh, yes, Miss Aldworth."

"And what would that be?"

"Many things, many, many things," he replied.

"Miss Marie." Delia touched her employer's white-gloved hand. "We are on our way to church."

"I am aware of that, Delia."

Delia gave the young Hargrave a hard glance. "I hardly think your mind is on our Heavenly Father. Is *yours,* Mr. Hargrave?"

"I—ah, beg your pardon, what did you say?"

"I was speaking of our Heavenly Father and the need for pious meditation before entering His house of worship."

Marie saw Hero's chagrined expression and bit her lip to keep from laughing.

"I hardly think we need be Puritans about it," Fannie said easily.

"I see no sign of the Puritan in the present company," Delia replied acidly.

"Darling Delia." Marie reached for her abigail's hand. "You must not make a piece of work about nothing."

"I wasn't aware that I was doing any such thing," Delia responded in hurt tones. "If you feel the Lord's day should be spent in frivolity and flirtation, I do not."

Fannie kept her eyes on the sour-faced woman across from her. "I promise you, Miss Dutton, I have no intention of engaging in any flirtations and I am quite sure Lady Agatha has no such thoughts either."

"Really!" Delia looked to Lady Agatha for support. That lady was gazing towards the village just ahead. "Lady Agatha, I cannot imagine that you condone this light behaviour that seems to surround us at the moment," Delia said, her head held high.

"Miss Dutton," Hero replied. "I assure you, there is nothing amiss."

"No? And just precisely how do you happen to know my mistress, Mr. Hargrave? You cannot have been formally introduced," Delia put in before Lady Agatha could speak.

"I introduced them," Fannie interjected.

Delia's arched brow told of her reaction to Fannie's words. "And you consider that a formal introduction?"

"Delia," Marie said, "please, that is enough."

"Is something amiss?" Lady Agatha asked, pulled back from her reverie by the feeling of tension in the air between the serving-women.

"Nothing's amiss," Fannie declared. As she spoke the driver slowed the matched chestnuts, the carriage coming to a stop in front of the small Wooster parish church in the midst of other carriages, buggies and simpler rigs. "We've arrived," she continued.

The Reverend Mr. Whipple greeted his new parishioners warmly, asking after Marie's father as Letty Merriweather came bustling up with Margaret and Charlotte Summerville and Captain Thomas Tompkins.

Charlotte gave Marie an appraising glance before turning to ask politely after Lady Agatha's health. Every now and then she cast a glance towards Hero and Marie.

"Captain Tompkins," Letty Merriweather said, "Miss Aldworth thinks you may be acquainted with her father, Major Daniel Aldworth."

"Aldworth, yes," Captain Tompkins replied. "By Jupiter, you can't be the pretty young thing who galloped about in cut-down trooper's trousers."

Marie laughed. "I fear I must confess." She saw the scandalised looks on the faces of the women surrounding her and laughed again, a little more self-conscious than she wanted to admit.

Delia, feeling the need of defending Marie's childhood, cast a quelling look towards her young charge as she spoke to the small assemblage. "Life on an army post is of necessity much less formal than normal society demands. I assure you Miss Marie was well-chaperoned at all times."

"I'll say she was," Captain Tompkins put in. "She had an entire regiment of chaperons!"

Charlotte Summerville gave Delia a thin little smile. "I must say, it sounds a most improper upbringing."

"Improper for a daughter to be closely watched by her father and his officers?" Fannie interjected. "I wouldn't know about that, having always lived in Dorset. And how is your current beau, Miss Charlotte? A viscount, I believe?"

"I hardly see the connection," Charlotte said in frozen tones.

"It's not formally announced yet but my darling Charlotte is engaged to the Marquess of Longworth," her mother put in, obviously relishing her news.

"How wonderful," Leticia said, with only the merest trace of disappointment that Margaret Summerville had kept this wonderful bit of news to herself. "Dear Charlotte, you must be so happy."

"I should say so," Fannie put in sweetly.

Charlotte gave Lady Agatha's abigail a withering glance before ignoring her remark and responding to the rotund widow Merriweather. "Thank you, *dear* Leticia. You have always been most kind."

"He is very handsome and his mother's uncle's cousin-by-marriage is twelfth in line to the throne," Margaret said proudly.

Hero Hargrave beamed as he spoke. "Capital, Charlotte! Who would have thought our own little Charlotte would end a titled lady?"

"I assure you, I did," Charlotte replied in syrupy tones.

"Well, then, you've done it," Hero applauded, "and none more deserving and all that."

"How sweet," Charlotte replied. She gave Marie another appraising glance. "And what a charming *new* companion you have found for yourself, dear Hero."

"My mistress is no one's companion, new or otherwise," Delia said, affronted.

"Miss Summerville meant nothing amiss," Hero assured Marie's abigail before he turned his full attention to her dark-haired mistress. "And I, for one, second her opinion. Miss Aldworth is *most* charming."

"The service is about to begin," Captain Tompkins informed the ladies. He bowed towards Agatha and offered his arm. "May I have the honour of escorting you, Lady Agatha?"

Margaret Summerville looked disappointed but smiled brightly as Hero offered his own arm, leaving Charlotte and Marie with Leticia Merriweather, and Fannie eyeing Delia Dutton. Fannie fell into step behind the others, her head held high as she followed her mistress towards the Steadford family pew.

The Reverend Whipple's sermon that Sunday dealt with the prodigal son, a topic that seemed of little interest to Hero

Hargrave. His eyes strayed to Marie over and over again as she attempted to ignore him. Marie sat farthest into the pew, Delia beside her. Fannie was between Delia and Lady Agatha, with Hero posted on the aisle seat, where his constant glances towards Marie attracted the attention not only of those sitting in the same pew but of those behind them as well.

"And his father said to his elder son, 'My son, your younger brother was dead and is alive again; he was lost and is found.' "

"How could this be true?" Reverend Whipple asked his flock. "Why did this father forgive his second son? This son who went to foreign lands and squandered his inheritance on low pursuits in dens of iniquity? Why did he call for his best robe for this son, why did he kill the fattened calf because this son was back safe and sound? Why?"

The clergyman's words rang out across the small church.

Fannie felt Agatha stiffen and gave her employer a sideways glance. She saw Lady Agatha's sudden paleness and felt the older woman's tension. The major is Henry Aldworth's son, Fannie thought suddenly. She said he never married but he did or he had a son in any event and she knows it.

The realisation that the new owner of the abbey was the son of the only man her mistress had ever loved brought Fannie up sharp. Without thinking, Fannie reached for Agatha's hand and gave it a little squeeze. She was rewarded by the strangest look she had ever seen upon her employer's face. Surprised that was very nearly consternation showed on the dowager's face. And something more. A softening, a fellow-feeling, as if to say she realised Fannie knew; as if to say we women are all, truly, sisters, under the skin. We can speak without words.

Fannie's life and heart and soul were bound to Agatha's, she had cared for and fretted over Agatha since she was a mere sixteen years old and sent upstairs to fetch and carry for the young chatelaine of Steadford Abbey. That was the year Lady Agatha's fourteen-year-old son ran away to war and it was Fannie who was beside Agatha late the next year when word came through that the boy had died on the ill-fated HMS *Victory*.

The news of her son's death devastated his mother. Agatha had taken to her bed, felled with a fever that nearly killed her and babbling words only Fannie heard. Homer Smyth was banished from his wife's rooms once Fannie realised her mistress was delirious, murmuring incoherent words that sometimes became clear. When they were clear they were about the man Agatha had loved, about the loss of love with him and now the loss of hope with her son dead.

Homer Smyth, rarely sober and never reasonable, was even less so as the years wore on. He seemed to feel the proper role for a male was to bully all those weaker than himself and curry favour with those who were stronger.

Since he was living off his wife's largesse at the time, Fannie formed early her opinions of the male of the species. The fact that they might be the supplicant, the receiver of the largesse, did not mean they would be grateful. In fact the reverse was true. They became more argumentative and nasty the more they received.

And they were no help during times of tragedy. Homer Smyth himself had stayed in London gaming and wenching when word first came of his son's death. Six years later, when their only daughter, Evelyn, was dying giving birth to young Jane, Homer was once again among the missing.

Father, mother, lover, son and daughter, all dead, before Agatha passed her fortieth year. Only her brother and the husband he had forced upon her were left. Lady Agatha had not taken to her bed when Evelyn died. The household staff gossiped that she had not been seen to shed a tear, but Fannie knew her mistress suffered more in silence than did many who wept and wailed their grief for all to see.

Lady Agatha had lifted her new granddaughter into her arms and had carried on, raising little Jane until the abbey was stripped from her by the chicanery of her brother and her husband. In the end good had come from the sale of the abbey, for the new owner had fallen in love with Jane and made her a duchess, even if he did take her far away to the New World.

The thought of Jane reminded Fannie that soon Jane and Charles and their little brood would be arriving home.

"Fannie?" Lady Agatha was calling her name for the second time. "The service is over."

Startled back into the present, Fannie jumped up from her seat, allowing Delia and Marie to follow the others from the Steadford pew and out into the October sunlight.

"Are you feeling unwell?" Agatha asked her servant.

"I'm fine," Fannie responded. "I was thinking about Jane and Charles arriving so soon and nowhere to put them."

"We'll manage," Lady Agatha replied.

"Yes, but how?"

Marie Aldworth touched Lady Agatha's sleeve. "If you have guests arriving, perhaps my father and I can help."

"Thank you, but we shall manage," Lady Agatha repeated.

Marie smiled at the elderly former owner. "But after all, the abbey has been your family home for generations. And my father and I use so very little of it. There are countless rooms simply going to waste. And I should so like to repay all your kindnesses in helping me ready the abbey for my father's arrival. Please at least consider our offer."

Lady Agatha took a moment studying the young woman before she replied. "Your father has not made any such offer."

Marie smiled wide. "Then I shall see that he does."

"Miss Aldworth?" Hero Hargrave came to draw the young beauty away, to speak to her alone.

Lady Agatha watched the young people move towards the shelter of an overhanging tree, the rest of Reverend Whipple's congregation swirling around, saying their goodbyes and going towards their carriages.

Fannie watched the direction of Agatha's gaze. "She is a lovely girl."

Agatha looked distracted. "Yes," she replied.

"But I can't say the same for her father," Fannie said plainly.

"You don't think he's good-looking?" Agatha asked, surprised.

Fannie sniffed. "Oh, he's good-looking enough but I say handsome is as handsome does. I'll wager he's no better than his father before him."

"I don't know what you're talking about."

"He's obviously Henry Aldworth's son and you know it." Fannie saw her mistress's face pale but she pushed determinedly on. "You may not want to face the fact that the man you loved married elsewhere and had children but you can hardly blame him, Aggie, you did the same yourself," Fannie pointed out.

"I did the same myself," Agatha agreed in a whisper.

"I think Major Aldworth has bought the abbey because his father told him of what happened all those years ago and how your father and brother behaved to him. The son is revenging himself upon the Steadfords and that's why he's cold as ice. He's judged us before even meeting us."

Lady Agatha looked distressed. "I do not wish to discuss this subject," she told Fannie.

"But—"

"Enough," Agatha said and Fannie unwillingly complied.

It was a silent journey back to the abbey for Agatha and Fannie. Hero seemed not to notice they did not contribute to the conversation, his attention upon Marie Aldworth as Delia kept silent and disapproving watch.

At the abbey, Hero hopped out to give his arm first to Lady Agatha, then to Marie, Fannie and Delia in turn.

"I think it might be best if we postponed our discussions," Lady Agatha began but Marie would hear none of it.

"Please don't desert me, Lady Agatha," Marie said. "I truly need your advice, I won't feel content unless I know you approve."

As they spoke the major came into view around the far corner of the abbey, striding towards them with a military gait. He drew nearer, a frown deepening as he saw the group.

"Papa." Marie ran towards him, giving him a quick kiss on the cheek. "Please," she said in lower tones, "you must persuade Lady Agatha to stay."

"I?" he questioned and then they were upon the others.

Delia gave a quick curtsey. "If you will excuse me."

Marie smiled at Lady Agatha. "We are going to return the abbey to its original decorations. Just as you remember it was."

"I do not think Sunday is the proper day to begin," Lady Agatha told Marie. She was turned away from Marie's father.

"And why not?" Daniel Aldworth asked.

Lady Agatha unwillingly met the younger man's gaze. "Sunday is meant to be the day of rest."

"I beg your pardon," he replied with a slight bow and a mocking tone. "Having lived my life in the army, I am unused to such niceties as days of rest. The enemy never saw fit to honour such occasions."

"You are home in England now," Lady Agatha pointed out, meeting Daniel Aldworth's almost insolent stare head-on.

"Thank you for reminding me," the major replied softly.

"If you wish to leave," Fannie interrupted, her anger rising at the impossible man's attitude, "I am ready, Lady Agatha."

Daniel Aldworth turned his gaze away from Agatha's dark and penetrating eyes to meet Fannie's insolent expression. "I thought Sunday might be a day Lady Agatha could spare you to work on the abbey records," he said.

Fannie gave the soldier a withering gaze. "I do not deal with anyone who is impertinent to my lady."

She was rewarded by a faint smile instead of the stinging retort she expected. Daniel Aldworth gave a slight bow to Lady Agatha's servant. "I shudder to think I have been impertinent. I did not intend so."

"Best bow to her ladyship and not to me," Fannie said with some little asperity.

"Fannie," Agatha said in deprecating tones, "enough."

"Not nearly enough, if you ask me," Fannie replied tartly.

Daniel bowed towards Lady Agatha, his expression decidedly less warm than it had been when he gazed upon Fannie Burns. "I am afraid, Lady Agatha, I have committed a grave solecism in your servant's eyes and I must apologise."

Fannie skewered the major with her eyes as well as her words. "The only apologies that truly count are those that are truly meant."

Daniel gave the serving-woman an enigmatic smile. "I assure you, I always truly mean what I say."

Fannie hesitated. She looked towards her mistress. "I had told Major Aldworth I could help him with the abbey accounts, if you agreed."

Marie came towards Lady Agatha, reaching for her arm. "What a wonderful idea. Whilst you are helping Papa, Lady Agatha can tell me more of the abbey's history. Please say you will," Marie ended.

"It appears I cannot very well decline," Agatha responded.

"Wonderful! Then it's settled," Marie said.

Hero stepped forward. "And may I be allowed to escort you both?"

"Who are you?" Daniel asked baldly. There was no welcome in his tone.

"Papa, this is Mr. Hieronymus Hargrave, but it seems all call him Hero."

"Why?" Daniel asked the younger man.

"I beg your pardon?" Hero's clear grey eyes looked puzzled. When Daniel did not reply, Hero sketched a quick bow in his direction. "Your servant, sir. And I assure you I have the most considerable interest in historical buildings such as the abbey."

"Do you now?" Marie asked impishly and then, seeing her father's expression, she reached for her papa's arm. "Mr. Hargrave is a very old friend of Lady Agatha's."

Her father did not seem impressed. "Miss Burns?" was all he said.

Marie drew Lady Agatha and Hero towards the door and into the entrance hall as Fannie stayed where she was and eyed the major.

"If you are ready, we can begin our work. The sooner begun, the sooner finished," he added after a brief pause.

"Good," Fannie said ungraciously. She marched inside, the new owner following close behind. "Are your manners common to all army officers?"

"I should think not," Daniel responded.

"That's a blessing," Fannie told him sharply.

As the last of the party disappeared inside the abbey, Sir Harry appeared at the round attic window above the portico, looking pensive and unsure.

ALL THAT SUNDAY afternoon Daniel Aldworth attempted to keep his attention upon his work with Fannie Burns. But the more he forced himself to his task, the more his mind would willfully wander away at the least noise from beyond the downstairs chamber in which he toiled over the account books with Lady Agatha's abigail.

"Is something amiss?" Fannie asked when she could stand his inattention no longer.

"No, nothing," came the reply.

"Perhaps you would have been better to go to church this morning," Fannie told him.

"I beg your pardon?"

"It's not my pardon you should be begging, but that of the Lord, himself."

Daniel Aldworth gave the abigail a bemused look. "Are you on such good terms with the Almighty that you deliver his pronouncements?"

"I've no need to do so," Fannie said sharply. "He is perfectly capable of taking care of all heathens."

"Heathens, is it? Because I do not attend the local church, am I to be branded an unbeliever?"

"There's many who would say so."

"I'm not asking the many. I'm asking Fannie Rose Burns."

Fannie felt the heat rising to her cheeks. "And I'm telling you the village will talk if the new owner of the abbey shuns his duties."

Daniel dismissed her words with a wave of his hand. "Idle minds always find something to talk about. I'm not concerned about them."

"And, pray tell, what are you concerned about then?"

Daniel studied Fannie's flushed face. "Your mistress, for one thing."

Fannie was taken aback. "My mistress?" she finally managed to say.

"Yes. How did she lose the abbey?"

Fannie's expression darkened. "That's family business, Major Aldworth, and not a pretty story."

"I have the time to hear it," he said mildly.

"It's a lesson in not trusting to the goodness of others. Not even your own flesh and blood."

Daniel Aldworth regarded the serving-woman for a long moment before replying. "I assure you, I am well aware of that lesson."

"Yes? Well, my lady has cause to rue the day she was born. Her father forced her into a loveless marriage, both her children died before her and her brother sold her home out from beneath her. What do you have to say to that?"

"You say both Lady Agatha's children died young?"

"A boy lost in the late war and a girl lost in childbirth. If it weren't for young Jane I don't know how she would have survived."

"Jane?"

"Her only granddaughter," Fannie replied.

Daniel's eyes narrowed. "And where is this granddaughter?"

"Across the Atlantic Ocean in America. Why do you ask?"

Daniel shrugged. "Merely curious."

"You seem very curious about Lady Agatha," Fannie told him.

"Do I? I suppose it's only natural. Steadfords seem to have owned the abbey for a very long time, judging by these records and the long lines of family portraits in the upper gallery. It seems strange a Steadford would willingly have let it go."

"And so it would if she had!" Fannie replied hotly. "It wasn't willingly on my lady's part, I can tell you, but there was naught to be done, even if little Jane did try to force her uncle to reconsider. It was my lady's odious brother, Nigel, who forced her out. She would not even have the gatehouse if not for Jane's husband, who insisted it be hers."

"And where was her husband through all this?" Daniel asked.

"In his grave and none too soon," Fannie said darkly. "We're not to speak bad of the dead but, if it weren't for Homer Smyth's gambling away my lady's portion to his crony Nigel, Steadford Abbey would still belong to a Steadford and the family would not be coming home to be shoved into the gatehouse's every nook and cranny."

Daniel frowned. "What do you mean, the family is coming?"

"Lady Agatha's granddaughter and her family are coming for her ladyship's birthday and, mayhap if we've luck, Sir Giles Steadford and his Elizabeth will be along too, although where we're to put them all, I've no idea." Fannie gave the obtuse man a long, penetrating gaze. "No idea at all," she added for good measure.

"Have you added the grain and seeds distributed to the tenant farmers each year?" Daniel Aldworth asked, his head bent to the record books, his interest in the Steadford family seemingly forgotten.

Fannie bit her lip. "Yes," she told the insensitive man. Feeling foolish, as if she had prattled on long past common sense, she picked up her pen and went back to her record-keeping.

Far away up the curving mahogany staircase, Lady Agatha stood with Marie Aldworth and Hero Hargrave in the long disused abbey nurseries on the topmost floor of the abbey, a bemused expression on her face.

"It is the same as it ever was," Lady Agatha said with a softened voice. Memories of the distant past coloured her words. "Except there are no children," she added sadly.

"Perhaps," Hero interjected, "that oversight can, in time, be corrected.

"Mr. Hargrave," Marie blurted out, her cheeks staining with deep red. "That is a most indelicate remark."

"I meant no disrespect," he assured. "But can you not see a family of little ones learning their sums, squealing, laughing and throwing their porridge about?"

"Porridge?" Sir Harry the Ghost materialised behind the threesome, glowering at the young people. "I'll throw enough porridge about for an army of brats if you young interlopers don't make yourselves scarce. I've few enough retreats without your messing about up here."

Hero Hargrave turned around. "I thought I heard—egad! What is that?"

Sir Harry found the young man staring directly at him. "And what do you think you're staring at?" Harry demanded. "If you'd been dead as long as me, you'd not look your best either."

Marie and Lady Agatha glanced back, their eyes suddenly riveted to the sight of a shimmering presence directly behind them.

"I . . . I think we are being visited by the famous abbey ghost," Hero said quietly, his awe in his voice.

"Oh, no." Marie's hand went to her breast. "He is real!"

The two young people were astonished but their shock was as nothing next to Sir Harry's own. He squinted towards them. "Is it possible you see me?" he asked and then his eyes went to Aggie's. She was staring at him. Staring at him full in the face. "Aggie?"

Agatha's face paled to ash, her hands beginning to shake. She tried to take a deep breath, the sound causing Marie to turn towards her.

"Lady Agatha!"

Harry heard Marie's tone. "Ah, Aggie-love, I've frightened you again, haven't I?" He spoke in saddened tones, a woebegone expression upon his face as he disappeared from view. Hero watched the vision fade, his brain feverishly trying to understand what had just transpired while he heard Marie's concern for Lady Agatha behind him. He forced his gaze away from where the ghost had been, turning in time to see Marie reaching to hold Lady Agatha up as the older woman's knees gave way beneath her.

"Lady Agatha, what's wrong?" Hero asked as he moved quickly to Agatha's other side, helping Marie as she brought the dowager to a wooden chair.

"I'm perfectly all right," Lady Agatha said faintly. "Or I shall be in a moment. I merely need to catch my breath. Perfectly all right," she repeated, more to herself than to them.

"I'll fetch Fannie, shall I?" Hero asked.

"Yes," Marie told him. "Go quickly, please." Marie knelt beside Lady Agatha's chair, touching her brow and then taking the dowager's hands within her own, chafing them and murmuring comforting words.

"Nothing to be afraid of," Lady Agatha said faintly. "A trick of the light."

"Yes, yes, of course," Marie said quickly. "You must take a deep breath, Lady Agatha, you look quite done in."

"Miss Marie?" Will Carston appeared in the doorway. "I passed a young gentleman who said you needed help." Taking in the situation at a glance, the major's batman came forward and knelt down beside Lady Agatha.

"There's no need for a fuss," she told them both.

"Of course not," Will replied. Turning to Marie, he said, "Should you loosen her stays?"

"Loosen my stays!" Lady Agatha's weakened voice rallied, scandalised. "I remind you, sir, I am a lady."

"Yes, ma'am."

"None have ever seen me with my stays loosened save myself and my abigail and none ever shall!"

"Yes, ma'am," Will Carston said again. "It's just that you need a chance to catch your breath."

Fannie and Hero arrived on the upper floor, accompanied by Daniel Aldworth. The sounds of their approach rose up the stairway and carried down the hall as Fannie questioned Hero about what had happened. Since his answer contained no concrete information, beyond Lady Agatha being frightened by a ghost, Fannie cut him off in midsentence.

"My lady has never in her life been frightened by anything, let alone by a nonexistent goblin. She's been overdoing, that's what the trouble is. She shouldn't be climbing stairs and tearing around the countryside at everyone's beck and call," Fannie complained, fear sharpening her words.

"I hope you don't feel we tired her," Hero said. "I simply hoped to offer a Sunday outing for her pleasure."

"You hoped to have a chaperon so that Major Aldworth would allow Miss Marie to accompany you to church," Fannie told him as she passed into the nursery ahead of Hero and the major. "What have you done to yourself, now?" Fannie asked in bracing tones as she went straight to her mistress, her fear and worry banished from her voice as she tried to rally the woman she had served for almost forty years.

Will Carston relinquished his place beside Agatha, his brow rising in response to the major's silent questions. Daniel stayed by the door, his attention upon Lady Agatha until the winds outside banged against a loose shutter.

The sound was loud in the quiet room. Daniel walked to the window, opening it and fastening the offending shutter into place. His back was to the room as he checked the two other windows. When he turned around, his expression darkened, his dark eyes focusing on some distant vista only he could see.

"Papa." Marie tugged at his arm. "We must see to a bed for Lady Agatha."

Major Aldworth heard his daughter's words. He looked past her to where Fannie stood beside Lady Agatha.

"I'm afraid Miss Marie has the right of it," Fannie said quietly. "I would rather not move her more than necessary."

"There's no problem at all, we have a score of empty rooms and all the will in the world to see Lady Agatha well again," Marie replied quickly. "Don't we, Papa?"

"Yes. Of course." Daniel sounded rather less forthcoming than his daughter.

"If you have any objections, we can—" Fannie began coldly but was stopped by Lady Agatha's own words.

"I have not yet crossed over," Agatha told the assemblage. "And I will thank you to remember that fact. Nor have I suddenly gone deaf. I am perfectly capable of—" Her words were interrupted by a need for a deep breath and the sinking feeling that she might very well soon faint.

She waved Fannie away. "Don't hover so. I think I will lie down for a bit, if Major Aldworth has no objection. Just for a moment before we leave."

"Of course, it's possible," Marie said quickly. "Will, if you and Mr. Hargrave will help, and Father," she added, casting him a swift glance, "we shall take Lady Agatha up to my rooms as they are already made up."

"I can manage alone," Will replied. "And it will be easier on the little lady."

"Little lady, indeed," Lady Agatha objected in a weakened voice. But she let the big man lift her into his arms.

Marie led the way to the next floor and the bedchamber that had long ago been Lady Agatha's own. As they descended, Delia came up the stairs from the ground floor, meeting them as they arrived at the chamber door.

"What's happened?" Delia cried.

"Nothing," Fannie said sharply. "My mistress just needs a few minutes rest and the use of the gig to get us home."

"Delia," Marie said, "please ask Hetty to make some tea and toast. A little sustenance," she continued to Lady Agatha as they neared her room, "and you will be on your feet."

Daniel Aldworth reached to open the door to the bed chamber and then checked on the threshold. He stepped back, silently allowing the others to precede him inside.

Agatha groaned as she was carried inside, the unexpected and unwelcome sound bringing Fannie crowding closer. "What ails you?" Fannie asked.

"Did you see something again?" Hero asked at the same time.

"This room," Agatha replied and then shut her eyes. "I had forgotten what Mary Beal had done to it."

Fannie did no more than glance at the garish oriental fantasy Mary Beal had created during her short reign as chatelaine of the abbey. "It suits her," Fannie said succinctly.

Marie had pulled the bed covers down and, now that Lady Agatha was ensconced on the large down bed, Marie reached to help Fannie undo the sensible black boots Lady

Agatha wore. "You must tell me how to restore the chambers to exactly as you had them. We want to make the abbey just as it was, don't we, Papa?" She looked back over her shoulder towards where her father stood. Still in the doorway, he was frowning, his gaze unreadable. "Just as it was," Marie continued, covering the silence that had greeted her words. "You must describe it all to the most tiny detail."

"However, not now," Fannie said pointedly.

"Oh no, of course not," Marie agreed.

Hero came near the bed and smiled down at the regal-looking woman who lay propped up on large feather pillows. "You'd best have a care lest I stay and keep you company."

"We shall all keep you company," Marie cried. "We shall have our tea right here."

"There's no need for such fripperies and fuss," Daniel Aldworth said from the doorway. The others turned towards him, startled by his choice of words. "She needs rest," he added.

"Major Aldworth is quite right," Hero put in. "We must leave and let Lady Agatha rest." Hero leaned closer to Marie. "We must talk about what we saw."

"Shhh," Marie whispered, her eyes going towards her father. "Not here."

Fannie remained as the others left. She fussed with the covers and pillows until Agatha cried halt.

"If you don't stop, you shall worry me to death," she told her abigail.

"And you never appreciating the half of what I do," Fannie said, trying to sound normal, trying to keep her worry away from her mistress's ears.

Evening shadows lengthened across the chamber a few hours later as Fannie dozed in a chair near the fire. Lady Agatha was still resting, her sleep fitful as she tossed and turned on the large bed across the room.

Hetty Mapes toiled up the servants' stairs with a tray of beef tea and a tisane, unwilling to let any of her helpers see to Lady Agatha's comfort. While she had breath in her body, she would tend to Lady Agatha herself, she told her minions and a few minutes later repeated the comment to Fannie, whispering about the benefits of her special tisane for Lady Agatha's strength and for her heart.

In the kitchen below young May, the scullery maid, looked from June's sad face to Margaret's and then to Delia Dutton's. "You'd think it was your very own mothers that were ill," the girl told the two older maids.

"I was thinking just the same, myself," Delia said.

June stared at the abigail. "It's our Lady Agatha that's ailing," she said as if that explained all.

"May's too young, and Miss Delia is too new to the abbey to understand," Margaret told June. She gave Marie's abigail a sympathetic smile. "When you've been here longer, you'll realise how very much Lady Agatha means to all of us."

"Why, we've grown up at the abbey and looking after Lady Agatha," June put in. "It wouldn't be the same without Steadfords at the abbey."

"There are no Steadfords at the abbey now," Delia pointed out.

"There is tonight," June said, her square chin jutting out pugnaciously.

"That's all right, then," Margaret said, smoothing the waters. "And we're here to work together, not to make arguments amongst ourselves."

"I still fail to see why you feel so much loyalty to the former owner," Delia repeated, determined to have the final word.

"I don't doubt it," June said succinctly.

Delia pressed her lips into a thin disapproving line. "I must say I am completely unused to such impertinence from the understaff."

Even the placid Margaret bridled at the new abigail's imperious tone. Hands on hips, she regarded the woman. "Well, then, Miss Delia, you'd best run along and report us both to Mr. Carston and Mrs. Mapes straightaway."

"I'm sure I have no intention of tattling about kitchen gossip to Mr. Carston."

"Good," June replied in a very definite tone. "You can just keep shut then, for your opinions aren't wanted in this kitchen."

"Well, I never!" Delia exclaimed.

"Yes, and you've never learned about proper loyalty either, it looks like to me," June added, warming to her subject.

"June." Margaret shook her head. "Lady Agatha wouldn't like our arguing."

June had her mouth open, ready to deliver her next jibe but, Margaret having found the only words that could have stopped her, she clamped her lips shut and turned back to her work.

Delia Dutton wished to find just the proper scathing reply but, all three backs being turned her way, she decided to retreat with head held high.

- *10* -

SUPPER WAS A quiet affair, Hero staying on, ready to transport Lady Agatha home to the gatehouse, and trying to make polite conversation at table while Delia Dutton served their food with pursed lips and a forbidding expression.

Daniel Aldworth was preoccupied, paying little attention to the dinner talk, answering only in monosyllables when he answered at all. Hero attempted to bring up the subject of the strange apparition but Marie interrupted his words with a negative shake of her head and a quick look towards where Delia stood by the sideboard.

Casting about for conversation, Hero asked about her life abroad. Marie launched into an animated discussion of the romance and the pitfalls of life amongst the military and the ins and outs of constantly setting up new establishments.

"You must find Dorset dismally provincial after living in such exotic climes," Hero said wistfully at the end of a particularly long description of the Spanish peninsula.

"Oh, no," Marie said in mellifluous accents, a smile lighting her dark eyes. "I am most excessively glad we have come to Dorset, I assure you. There are so many agreeable things about the abbey and its neighbours."

Hero smiled back. "I hope I am included in the agreeable neighbours."

Marie cast him a roguish smile from beneath her eyelashes. "There are so few I have met," she answered, flirting outrageously.

Hero's smile widened. "You must let me help remedy that oversight by escorting you upon your morning calls. I am acquainted with the entire county, Miss Aldworth, and I intend to persuade you to be even more glad of your father's decision to retire to Steadford Abbey."

"What was that you said?" the man in question asked Hero, his attention coming to rest on the young man's face.

Hero was startled at the major's sudden interest in the conversation. "I was merely telling your daughter I hope she will find her new life in Dorset to her liking."

Daniel's eyes clouded over. "I pray she may find more joy of this county than the rest of her family have."

"Sir?" Hero Hargrave was perplexed by the major's cryptic words.

"Nothing." Daniel stood up. "If you will excuse me, I must see to . . ." He hesitated. "Our guest's comfort," he finished.

"If you have need of me, Papa, I shall come too."

"Finish your meal first," he replied as he left.

Hero watched the young woman's eyes cloud with worry. "I am convinced Lady Agatha will be fit as ever once she rests."

"I sincerely hope so. She is such a dear. I could not have had the house in readiness for my father's arrival if not for her help. It is no wonder the staff is so devoted to her." Marie heard Delia sniff from her position by the sideboard and turned towards the serving-woman. "Dear Delia, you have been doing double duty for so long I am quite ashamed. You must go see to your own supper."

"And leave you alone with a man?" Delia responded astounded. "I would never commit such a solecism."

Mary smiled sweetly. "Then will you please send for the tea tray. Mr. Hargrave has expressed a desire to have it at table, since we are, as you say, alone."

Mr. Hargrave, who had expressed no such desire, looked a bit surprised but kept his questions to himself. Delia went through the green baize door and Marie turned to Hero, speaking quickly. "She'll not leave us alone long. Did you see what frightened Lady Agatha?"

Hero was unwilling to sound foolish, but curiosity warred with prudence. Curiosity won. "Something transparent?" he ventured uneasily.

"Exactly!" Marie cried. "Something almost totally transparent and most definitely, I believe, in the form of a man."

"In tattered robes that look a hundred years old?"

"Or older. Yes." Marie whispered the word. She took a deep breath and then rushed on. "Mr. Hargrave, I must tell you I've seen him before."

"By Jupiter, have you really?"

"I am now quite positive of it," she replied excitedly.

"I say, do you think he might be the abbey ghost they've talked about all these years?"

Marie's eyes grew large. "Oh, I hope so. But how can we be sure?"

"There's nothing for it, we must contrive to see him again." The more Hero thought about it, the more he warmed to the adventure.

"But how can we? I very much doubt he would come if we should call him. Besides, I've already tried."

Hero looked shocked. "You have? Egad, but you're a brave one, aren't you, for a girl."

"I beg your pardon," Marie replied, a little put out at his tone.

He made amends quickly. "Miss Aldworth, I have the highest respect for your person and the deepest admiration for your daring, I assure you. I confess I've never met a female such as yourself in all of London and Dorset combined."

"And I assure you, Mr. Hargrave, that after growing up in the midst of the French wars I have no fear left in me, let alone fear of transparent men."

"Capital!" he exclaimed. "That means you'll join my search."

"Oh, no!"

"I thought you were not afraid."

"Of ghosts, I'm not. Delia's wrath is another matter altogether. There is no hope she would condone our racketing about the abbey alone and I am quite, quite sure she would not take to a ghost. She would give him a good talking to and then he would leave and we should never find out his story."

"Then we must search for him in secret."

"Delia will not like it."

"We shall convince her I've left and then I shall meet you in the nursery."

"There is no way," Marie said practically.

"Ah, but there is. There is a secret stairway that leads from the west terrace to the master's room." He saw her surprise and spoke in a conspiratorial tone. "It was put there by monks when the Tudors kept changing their minds about religion and it was used only a few years ago when the Beal girls got married right here in the abbey chapel."

"Truly?"

"Oh, we had an excellent adventure. Lady Agatha was a trump, helping Becky Beal to marry her Paul whilst all the time everyone thought only Alice and Andrew were getting married. Andrew is a good friend of mine and he shall soon be coming for Lady Agatha's birthday. It was great fun, I can tell you. And there was much talk of the ghost then but dashed if I ever saw it. Now I have my chance!"

"Hush, I hear Delia coming back."

His voice dropped to a whisper. "I shall make a big show of leaving and then will meet you as soon as ever I can in the nursery."

"We can't! It's much too late."

Hero nodded unhappily. "You may have the right of it." He brightened. "I have it, I shall ride over tomorrow afternoon and we shall meet then. In the nursery," he added.

"I—" Marie began to object but Delia was upon them and she had no chance to say more.

Delia brought word that Lady Agatha would be staying the night; her lips pressed together primly after she delivered herself of this knowledge.

Hero took his cue and quickly took his leave, barely finishing the tea Delia had brought him. He did not wait upon the major's return from the nether regions of the house but begged Marie to give her father his regrets. He gave Delia Dutton as well as Marie a very pretty bow and was gone in a flurry of movement and words.

Delia saw her mistress's expression and took it for disappointment. "He stayed entirely too long, as it was," Delia pronounced.

"He was waiting for Lady Agatha," Marie defended.

"Anyone could see she was going nowhere this night," Delia responded tartly.

Marie ignored this jibe. "I think I shall look in upon Lady Agatha before I retire."

"I'll lay out your things," Delia said, coming behind.

"No," Marie said too quickly. "That is, I really think you should see to Miss Fannie's comfort and Lady Agatha's. I am quite capable of seeing to my own needs this one night."

"You're not even in your own room this night. I had the front spare room made up for you and a fire laid on, as I was positive her ladyship would be staying the night. I must say, you have been in the most peculiar mood today," Delia told Marie.

"I don't know what you mean," came the reply.

"You're not yourself these days. Nor is your father, if the truth be known."

"Both Papa and I are perfectly all right and I, myself, shall be just fine this night," Marie said firmly. "I am not a child that can't undo her own hairpins and find a night-gown in a strange room. We've made ourselves comfortable in many unfamiliar surroundings over the years, including tents, as I remember."

"I disremember many tents," Delia declared stoutly.

"Good night, dear Delia." Marie reached to give her abigail a quick peck on the cheek and then lifted her skirts and ran up the stairs towards the Long Gallery overhead.

"Something havey-cavey's going on around here," Delia said darkly as she watched her mistress go.

Marie made it to the comparative safety of the chamber she would use that night and closed the door, leaning against it as she took great gulps of air. Her heart was racing. The drawn curtains on the far side of the unfamiliar room rustled softly and she turned to stare at them.

With slow steps she went towards the window, preparing to see a vision suddenly appear, but all she found was a not quite closed window letting in the cold night air in little gusts. Marie latched the window and turned back towards the fire, warming herself before changing into her nightclothes.

Across the hall Daniel stood in the middle of his own chamber, allowing Will Carston to help him into his nightrobe and slippers.

"Has everything been seen to?" Daniel asked.

"Yes, sir. Timothy brought the bits and pieces Miss Fannie asked for from the gatehouse and she said as how they had all they needed for the night."

"Good. You may go, then."

"Very well, sir."

Daniel stood where he was, listening as Will crossed the master's sitting-room and let himself into his own small room. Once alone, Daniel looked towards the connecting door that led to the rooms Lady Agatha and Fannie were using. He hesitated and then walked forward, hesitating again with his hand on the knob. He tapped and waited. There was no response and, after another moment, he tried the knob. It turned, the door opening into a tiny hall that led past a dressing room to the room where Lady Agatha lay.

The major moved slowly, not wishing to disturb her sleep. The door to his daughter's large chamber was open, the flickering of the waning fire an uncertain light in the shadowy room. Lady Agatha was asleep, the sound of gentle snoring coming from the large bed.

Daniel watched the elderly woman for a long moment until Fannie Burns made a little sound. He glanced towards the fireplace to see Fannie shifting in her chair, her eyes closed, her breathing steady.

The major walked forward until he was beside Lady Agatha's servant. He stood quietly for another long, full minute before he leaned over to gently touch her shoulder.

"Miss Burns," he whispered.

His touch and his voice brought her awake, startled and a bit disoriented at first. "What—?"

"Shhh," he warned and cocked his head towards the bed across the room. "You'll wake her."

Fannie rubbed her eyes. "What do you want?"

"I want you to rest on the bed Delia made up for you."

"I'm fine where I am."

"You are most definitely not fine," he whispered. "Nor should this conversation take place in here." He stepped back, waiting for her to stand. When she did, it was slowly. She favoured the cramped muscles in her back and legs and grimaced when she saw his expression.

When they reached the sitting-room he was lighting a candle. "She should not be left alone," Fannie said.

"I will see that someone stays with her and I will see that you are called if there is the least bit of change. Now it is time for you to get some rest or you will be of no help to her when she wakes up and needs you."

His logic was hard to dismiss and, bone-tired, Fannie allowed herself to be led from the sitting-room to the chamber that had been readied next door, the major's candle lighting the way.

"We must apologise for putting you to such trouble," Fannie told him.

He shrugged. "I trust she will be well," he said as he opened the door for her.

"She has to be," Fannie replied firmly as she went inside.

There was an awkward moment when Fannie, standing just inside, realised her host was in his nightclothes and alone with her in the fire-lit room. Suddenly she found she was uncomfortably warm.

"If there is nothing further you need," he was saying.

"No. Nothing. Thank you."

"I believe Delia had your things brought here."

"I am quite sure everything necessary has been done," Fannie replied. She was irritated at herself for feeling self-conscious. Inwardly castigating herself for acting like a silly young chit of a girl, her unease communicated itself to the major.

"I shall leave you then," he said.

"Thank you and—good night," Fannie replied.

He gave her a searching look, the sharp planes of his face highlighted by the play of light and shadows from the candle he held. His eyes were dark as night and mesmerizing.

"I shall leave you this," he said, handing the candle over by the round brass ring of its holder.

"Thank you, again," Fannie said, reaching for it. Their fingers brushed. Startled by her own nervousness, she closed the door behind him, her heart thudding against her breastbone, and told herself she must be coming down with a cold.

She did not know that Daniel Aldworth himself took her place in the chair by Lady Agatha's fire and waited out the dark hours until dawn keeping vigil.

11

THE NEXT MORNING Fannie woke with the sun shining in her eyes from an unfamiliar angle. It was a moment before she remembered where she was and sat up. The fire in the grate had long since gone out; even the ashes were cold and the chill air did her stiff limbs no favour. She forced herself to her feet, grimacing at the signs of oncoming age. When she was young she had hopped out of bed with no thought to the movement of joints and muscles.

For some unknown reason the thought of youth made her hark back to the previous night, waking in her chair to see Major Aldworth standing over her, staring down at her with hooded eyes. And with that she thought of her ladyship in the next room.

Fannie reached for the change of clothing young Tim had brought up from the gatehouse and quickly performed her morning ablutions in the freezing cold water of a flowered porcelain pitcher and washbowl. When she was finished she hurried towards Lady Agatha's side.

A bleary-eyed Daniel Aldworth looked up from the chair by the fire-place that Fannie had vacated the night before.

Startled to see him there, she lost the distrustful look he had grown used to, her expression softening as she questioned him with her eyes. He put his finger to his lips and she looked across the room to where Lady Agatha still slept. Fannie went near the bed, peering down at her mistress. Satisfied that all was well, she motioned to the major to follow her and waited patiently and a bit pointedly at the sitting-room doorway.

Daniel thought about staying where he was but the kind, even grateful, look in Fannie's eyes changed his mind. He heaved himself out of the chair and followed her into the next room.

She could see how tired he looked. "Major Aldworth," Fannie began in a gently reprimanding tone, "please tell me you did not take over my duties when you sent me off to bed last night."

"Of course not," came the reply.

His words gave the abigail pause. She took a deep breath and went on, determined to clarify the situation. "Then I am to take it, you did not spend last night in the very chair you wrested from me?"

"I believe I have already answered that question." Feeling rather self-conscious under her gaze, Daniel spoke with raised brow and a condescending tone guaranteed to irritate Fannie past endurance.

Quick anger surged within Fannie's normally phlegmatic bosom. Determined not to let the big oaf know he had irritated her, she raised her head high. "If you'll excuse me, I shall see to my lady's comfort."

Daniel Aldworth watched Lady Agatha's serving-woman walk away. He had accomplished his purpose and ended her questions but his success saddened him; he wanted to reach out and stop her, to tell her the truth about his all-night vigil. She left the room, his chance for honesty gone, and he felt the poorer for his choice.

Across the hall, Marie awoke and sat up in almost the same moment, the morning light bringing with it the memory of Hero's plan. He was sure to be discovered as he crept up the secret stairs and skulked about in her father's rooms and her father would most likely run him through with his sword and then where would they all be? Picturing the catastrophes that would befall if her father stumbled upon Hero, Marie dressed quickly, determined to stave off any confrontation between Hero and her father. As she hurried through her morning toilette she framed a hundred excuses to give her father if they were caught. Each sounded less likely than the one before.

She opened her bedchamber door just as her father closed the door to Lady Agatha's rooms and started down the hall. Marie ducked back inside her door.

"Marie?" Daniel called out. He sounded very tired and more than a little short-tempered.

Unwillingly Marie came out into the hall. She tried to mask her unease and gave her father a quick kiss on the cheek. "Good morning, Papa."

"What are you up to, young lady?"

"I don't know what you can mean, Papa."

"I mean, whatever it is that's making you hop from one foot to the other so impatiently. But whatever it is, it can wait until I wake."

"Until you wake?" she asked weakly. "Are you thinking of going back to bed? I mean, it's such a beautiful morning, I should think a good brisk ride would be just the thing."

"Then I suggest you apply to Will to accompany you and take one. I am going to get some rest. Before you go, stop in and see if Lady Agatha needs anything." Too weary to deal with his obviously agitated daughter, he walked away.

With sinking heart Marie watched him go. When he opened the door to his rooms she held her breath and closed her eyes, imagining her father walking straight into a dark figure in his bedchamber and running him through before he realised it was Hero Hargrave. Marie's eyes flew open. Even if her father saw who it was he might run him through on general principles. Her father was very strict about proper procedures, protocol and principles. Marie blamed it on a life spent in the army, but there it was and how she could ever explain ghosts and secret stairs to her father she had no idea.

Into her anxious thoughts came the realisation that no shouts, no sounds of fisticuffs or sabres were emanating from her father's chambers. Not even a questioning voice. Marie took a deep breath and turned back along the hall to do as her father had bid and see to Lady Agatha's comfort. Perhaps Mr. Hargrave had changed his mind or perhaps he had forgotten the adventure entirely. She tried to tell herself she was very glad if he had, but a tiny bit of disappointment remained as she tapped on the door to her own rooms, where Lady Agatha now lay resting.

Fannie opened the door and stepped out into the hall beside Marie, answering her questions in a whisper. "I can't remember when she's slept so late," Fannie told Marie, "but she seems to be comfortable."

"We shouldn't disturb her then," Marie replied. "Papa asked me to see if there was anything you needed."

"He did, did he?" Fannie's concerned expression took on a decidedly pink cast in the soft morning light from the mullioned windows beyond them in the Long Gallery. If Marie hadn't known better, she would have sworn Fannie was blushing. "I would be grateful if you could sit with her for a few minutes. I want to remind Hetty her ladyship's very particular about her eggs when she wakes. It's been a deal of years since Hetty has fixed her breakfast eggs and tea."

"Of course." Marie reached out to touch Fannie's arm. "I am sure her ladyship will soon be right as rain."

Fannie smiled at the pretty young woman. "I was thinking the very same thing."

"You must not worry a bit and you must stay as long as you like, you know. We are glad to have you both."

"Thank you, Miss Marie. That means a great deal, it truly does, and not only to her ladyship."

"I'll sit and keep her company until you return."

"I'll only be a moment," Fannie replied as she sped towards the servants' stairs.

Marie watched until the green baize door at the end of the hall fell shut behind the abigail. Then she went inside the bedroom and sat down in the chair by the fire, staring across the room at the ancient carved bed where Lady Agatha lay sleeping. It had been Lady Agatha's for long, long years and now it was Marie's. It was a daunting thought for the young woman, almost as if she, herself, were the interloper, as if Lady Agatha belonged in these rooms more truly than could any other.

Marie tried to sit quietly, tried not to fidget, but she started at every sound from beyond the bedchamber, afraid it was Hero sneaking about. Perhaps, she thought hopefully, if he did come he would see her father asleep in his bed and go back the way he came.

She tried to picture the reckless young man, who had swept an unknown, nightgowned female off her feet and onto his horse, behaving in a cautious manner. Visions of his delight at the idea of a ghost hovering about the abbey welled up. It didn't seem very likely the impetuous Mr. Hargrave would meekly decide against his quest to find the abbey's supernatural guest.

The memory of the ghostly figure's appearance chilled through Marie, her gaze straying back towards the sleeping Lady Agatha. When she awoke, perhaps she could shed light on the questions that intrigued both Marie and Hero.

Marie's hopes were not to be realised that morning, since Lady Agatha slept quietly and late. Meanwhile Marie's father took what little rest he could in the rooms next door, his dreams more troubled than he would have liked to admit.

Fannie brought up her ladyship's breakfast late in the morning. She shared it with Marie and they played Double Patience at a small cherrywood table in the sitting-room next to where Lady Agatha slumbered.

At each and every untoward sound in the hall and rooms beyond, Marie jumped. Fannie looked more and more askance as Marie's excuses wore more and more thin. The morning lengthened towards noon, Fannie eyeing the girl carefully, trying to decide what was wrong with her.

"You're sure you are feeling quite well?" Fannie asked.

"Yes," Marie replied swiftly. "Yes," she repeated. "Of course."

Fannie was going to say more but sounds of wakefulness came from the inner chamber. She went to Lady Agatha as Marie saw her chance and escaped to the hall. Seeing no one near, Marie stopped at the door to her father's sitting-room.

Delia Dutton, coming through the green baize door at the back of the upper hall, was greeted by the sight of her young mistress leaning with one ear to her father's sitting-room door. "Miss Marie?" Delia said, startling the younger woman. "Is anything wrong?" she asked in disapproving accents.

"What? No. No," Marie replied with even more vehemence. "Of course not."

A sound came from behind them, either from along the Long Gallery or in the major's apartment. Marie strove to appear nonchalant as Delia turned towards the noise.

"Did you hear that?"

"No. What? I heard nothing," Marie replied.

Delia started towards the gallery, the master's suite directly ahead. "I could swear I heard something," Delia said.

"Delia Dutton, this is a large house," Marie said impatiently. "Surely you have heard *something* at every moment since we first arrived! I don't know why you should be particularly interested in odd sounds this morning when they've been heard from morning to night ever since we arrived and most likely long before!"

Delia's brow scrunched into questioning lines as she looked at the girl she had raised very nearly by herself. "There's no need for such vehemence," Delia replied mildly. "I must say, it's quite out of character for you, Miss Marie."

"I don't know what you mean," Marie responded sharply.

Delia thought of many tart answers but said none of them. "If you have no need of me, I'm sure I have many things to occupy my time," she said in hurt tones.

"Then you'd best go along and see to them," Marie replied and then, feeling guilty, she tried to lighten the moment and smiled. "I can do perfectly well on my own."

Delia sniffed and raised her pointed chin. "If you say so," she answered.

Marie watched Delia walk away. Once the abigail had disappeared downstairs, Marie sped towards her father's rooms, more terrified with every step. At the door she thought about knocking but decided against it and gently turned the knob, opening the door.

The room was silent and empty. Marie slipped inside, tiptoeing towards her father's inner chamber with bated breath. She was very sure Hero Hargrave must have considered the dangers, the impossibility, of his proposed adventure and, having done so, would reach the same conclusions she had. Surely he must decide against attempting anything so foolish since the game was not worth the candle.

Marie was quite right in her assessments of the situation but, unfortunately, Hero was not privy to them and so, when he ducked his head out of the clothespress, he was greeted with the sound of Major Aldworth snoring on his bed and the sight of the major's daughter staring at him, horrified, from the doorway beyond.

Marie had the sense to stop her gasp before it woke her father. She stepped back into the sitting-room, stiffening as she heard Hero's movements across the inner room. At every moment she expected her father to wake and find them there. When Hero appeared in the sitting-room doorway she very nearly fainted but, pulling herself together, she motioned him forward and out of the lion's den.

The hallway beyond was only slightly less perilous. Marie moved swiftly towards and up the stairs, all the while praying Hero would keep up. He did and soon they were closeted in the empty nursery, Marie's hand pressed to her waist as she gasped, trying to catch her breath and calm her racing heart.

"We've made it, Miss Aldworth, there's no need to worry now," Hero said in his best bracing manner.

"No need to worry?" Marie responded, dumbfounded at the man's lack of understanding.

"What I meant to say is that we are safe."

"Not if any hear us or come near. If my father finds you've sneaked into the abbey he will be most fearfully angry at both of us."

"We could tell him the truth," Hero offered.

"Mr. Hargrave, that is the very last thing we could do! I assure you my father would not take kindly to having a ghost in his house, nor would he feel such a possibility was good enough reason for our being up here unchaperoned."

Hero grinned. "At least this time you are fully clothed," he said.

Reminded of the morning they met, Marie's dark eyes blazed as scarlet stained her cheeks. "A *gentleman* would not bring up such a subject."

"I did not mean to annoy you. I thought you were most fetching in your . . . *dishabille*."

Marie stiffened. "You are impertinent, sir."

Hero heard Marie's indignation and attempted to look the picture of contrition as he apologised and changed the subject. "After all," he continued, "we are here because of what we saw and what you had seen before. How do you suggest we call the ghost?" Hero asked.

Marie swallowed. "I am not quite sure. That is to say, I don't know."

"How did you persuade him to appear before?"

"I did nothing. I think it was his idea," she replied quietly, their quest suddenly very real in the silent nursery rooms. "Do you think perhaps he truly exists?"

"*Something* exists and I intend to find it," Hero said in most definite accents. But after hours of poking into dusty corners he was less enthusiastic.

"He may not be appreciative of our intruding upon his solitude," Marie said as they sat upon a brass-bound trunk staring around the cluttered attic. "Perhaps we should leave well enough alone."

"Since we can't see him, I hardly see how we can be intruding upon his privacy," Hero replied practically. "I wonder what one must do or say to call a ghost?"

"I rather assumed he would just appear. As he did before," Marie explained.

"Hardly likely," Hero said. "I mean why would he?"

"Why did he before?" Marie asked.

"I wish I knew," came a gruff reply.

"Hero? I mean, Mr. Hargrave?"

"Please, I like Hero much better."

"Did you just—by any chance—speak?"

"No," Hero replied.

"Did you . . . hear . . . someone speak?" Marie asked.

"I thought I heard something but—by gad! Do you think it's here?"

"Of course I'm here," Sir Harry the Ghost replied irritably. "And I'm not an it, I'm a he. Which brings me to why *you* are wandering about up here. I have precious little to call my own," he groused, "without you humans tramping about in my last refuge where you have no need to be."

"Oh, my," Marie said.

"Oh, my, what?" Harry asked.

Marie swallowed. "Oh, my, I fear you truly are a ghost."

"And what else would I be in this sorry state?" Sir Harry demanded.

"Oh, I say," Hero breathed the words as he stared in awe at the half-transparent figure halfway across the room. "Are you *truly* a ghost?"

Harry looked towards Marie. "Is there something wrong with him? Attic a bit queer?"

"I beg your pardon?" Hero said.

"And well you should," the ghost opined.

"Yes, but, well, dash it, I beg your pardon?" Hero said again in rather more agitated tones.

"You already said that," Marie pointed out.

"I know what I said," Hero retorted irritably. "I just don't know what he meant."

Harry scowled at the two young people. "At least you've got the good grace to admit your ignorance, which is more than can be said for most of the human race."

"Mr. Ghost," Marie said, "we are not merely curious, you understand. That would show a fearful lack of manners even with a—I mean, even under the present circumstances."

"I know exactly what you meant," Harry told her.

"You see, we weren't sure. That is to say, we needed to ascertain if you were, in fact, real. As it were."

"Why?" Harry growled.

"Why?" Marie faltered.

"You heard me," Harry said. "Other than idle curiosity, why did you need to do any such thing?"

"Actually," Hero began, "it was rather more from curiosity than anything—"

"Mr. Hargrave!" Marie tried to wither the young man with her glance. "I hardly think you need be so impolite," she told him sharply. "Especially since this was your idea in the first place and he is, after all, *our* ghost!"

"I'm no one's ghost but my own and you'd bloody well better know it now," Harry roared and was rewarded with two very chastised expressions.

Marie gulped. "It's because of Lady Agatha," she said quickly.

"What?" Sir Harry came towards the young woman, concern written large across his pale features. "What's wrong with Aggie?" he demanded.

"We're not quite sure," Marie began.

"She felt quite faint after seeing you," Hero put in.

"Don't you think I know that?" Harry bellowed. Then almost at once his anger collapsed, his expression turning distant and glum. "I've stayed away so I wouldn't disturb her."

"I'm sure you didn't mean to worry her," Marie began, only to be silenced by Harry's next words.

"Of course I didn't mean to worry her," he thundered, his voice rising with each word. The two humans blanched, the sight somewhat mollifying the ghost's bad temper. "You'd best have a care," Harry said darkly. "Both of you," he put in for good measure.

"Quite so," Hero said.

"We shall," Marie agreed.

"Good," Harry told them both. "How is my Aggie?"

"She was sleeping when I left," Marie said.

"I wish I could see her," Sir Harry said forlornly.

"Couldn't you perhaps go through the wall or something?" Hero asked helpfully. He earned a disdainful ghostly look.

"Of course I can go through walls. What kind of ghost do you take me for? But if she sees me, or senses I'm there, I'll only make her worse."

"Hasn't she seen you before?" Hero asked. "I mean, you've not just arrived, have you? You would seem to have been a ghost for quite a long time, judging by your clothes."

"What's wrong with my clothes?" Harry thundered.

"Nothing," Hero said hastily. "I'm sure they were the height of fashion when—when you first wore them."

"Young man, I'd like to see *you* manage for decades with no new apparel and no valet."

"I'm sure it must be devilish awful. Could put one into quite the most awful tweak, sir."

"It can and it does," Harry retorted.

"So you do know each other? Lady Agatha and you?" Hero asked a bit recklessly. "Having been in such close proximity for—for how many years, sir?"

"More than you need know of," Harry said.

Marie took a step nearer the ghost. "Perhaps you really *should* go to her. It might be just the thing to revive her, don't you think?"

Harry turned his full attention to the dark-haired beauty, hope dawning. "Do you truly think so?"

"Yes, I do," Marie said in her most positive tone. "Why don't you just go and see?"

"I'm afraid."

The ghost's words disconcerted his hearers. Silence hovered over the empty nursery until Marie, softly, broke it.

"Mr. Ghost, why should you be afraid of Lady Agatha?"

"I'm afraid I'll hurt her," Harry said bleakly.

Marie took another single, tentative step towards the apparition. "Perhaps she won't see you. After all, you don't have to let her see you, do you?"

Harry looked glum. "I ranted for all these years because she couldn't see me and now that she can, I'm afraid to show myself for fear of hurting her."

"You mean," Hero put in, "she'd never seen you?"

"Not until this very week," Harry replied.

"No wonder she was so upset." Hero thought about it. "But—if she's never seen you, why can she now?"

"I'll be damned if I know," the ghost told the handsome young man. "Only those who are in love have ever been able to see me."

"But Lady Agatha is not in love," Marie said.

"More to the point, neither are we," Hero added.

Sir Harry perused one young face and then the other. "You may think not, but rest assured you are. Only lovers have ever seen me in this state and it's only by lovers that my penance can be worked out."

"What penance?" Marie asked.

Sir Harry grimaced. "It's a long story."

"Marie, I mean, Miss Aldworth, did you hear what this—this—gentleman said? He said we must be in love."

Marie dismissed Hero's words with a wave of her hand. "He said all who see him must be in love, but surely Lady Agatha does not have a *tendre* for someone, and so he has the wrong end of it, that's all."

"Are you so very sure?" Sir Harry asked. He earned a long and searching gaze from young Marie. And a questioning one from the handsome Hero. "Both of you?" he continued.

Marie could not answer the apparition's questions but she caught his attention and held it with her words. "Is there some history between you and Lady Agatha, Mr. Ghost?"

Harry thought about prevaricating but, in the end, simply told the truth. "Yes."

"Might she be glad of your presence?" Marie asked.

Harry's answer was a long time coming. "I don't know."

"Then," Marie said softly, "perhaps you'd best find out. If you truly care about her."

"Truly care about her!" Harry bellowed and then, seeing Marie's understanding gaze, he relented. "Truly care," he said again and then, finally, he added, "I'll go and see." As he spoke he disappeared.

Hero's grey eyes were large with questions. "Egad, I think the bloody thing is actually bloody real."

"Mr. Hargrave!" Marie exclaimed. "Real or no, there is no need for such excessive swearing."

"Begging your pardon, of course, dear Marie."

"You must not call me so," she reprimanded. But she did not sound terribly displeased.

"And what if our ghost has the right of it?" Hero persisted. He reached for her hands and held them within his own. "What if we are meant to be lovers?"

"I—I don't know what you mean." Marie tried to disengage both her hands and her emotions but neither obeyed her. He drew her slowly towards him, Marie watching as his head descended, his lips coming to meet hers.

12

"MR. HARGRAVE!" MARIE gasped as Hero released her.

"Don't you think you might now call me Hero?" he asked.

"I cannot imagine calling you Hero," she replied, vinegar in her tone.

"Then perhaps Hieronymus?" he offered helpfully.

"Even less so," she told him. Her beautiful face was set into prim lines. "I should never have agreed to this adventure," she informed the impertinent young man. She started down the steps with a determined stride, Hero following and catching up as she reached the first floor hall.

"Please, wait," he said.

"Absolutely not," she said but even as she spoke, she slowed. "You have exceeded all bounds, sir."

He reached for her hand. "Ah, but Miss Aldworth, you are such a sweet temptation."

Marie regarded his twinkling grey eyes. "Are you laughing at me?"

"Heavens no," came the reply, but his expression was so merry it gave the lie to his words.

"I think you are," she told him plainly. "And I don't like it one little bit. Release my hand this very instant."

"But I like holding your hand."

"From our very first meeting you have shown the most atrocious of manners, not to say absolute cheek, Mr. Hargrave. I hardly know what's to be done with you."

"If I might suggest?" Hero said and with that he drew her near and kissed her again.

"Miss Marie!" Delia's shock rang out along the corridor, startling the two young lovers. They sprang apart as the redoubtable Miss Dutton bore down upon them, eyes blazing. "What is the meaning of this?"

"Mr. Hargrave has come to see how Lady Agatha is," Marie said quickly.

"Up here?" Delia demanded. "Without being announced?"

"You see," Hero began but he was stopped midsentence by Marie's next words.

"You see, I—I was just going out when he arrived," Marie told her abigail. "There's no need to make such a fuss."

"No need, indeed," Delia said, scandalised by Marie's want of proper conduct. "I'm sure I didn't raise you to be kissing strangers on backstairs!"

"Actually, we're nowhere near the backstairs," Hero put in and earned a nasty glance from their interlocutor.

"Come along!" Marie dragged Hero towards the chamber Lady Agatha occupied, Delia coming right behind them.

"I've looked for you all afternoon, Miss Marie. It's almost dinnertime," Delia pointed out with absolutely no welcome in her voice at all.

"Capital," Hero replied. He glanced back to give the stern-looking woman a dazzling smile. "I wondered why I was so famished."

"I was not aware you had been invited to dinner," Delia retorted sharply.

"Delia, that's terribly rude," Marie objected. "Please tell Cook Mr. Hargrave will be staying at dinner."

Delia gave her mistress a dark look. "Major Aldworth will hear of this."

"Since he will undoubtedly join us for dinner, I'm sure he will," Marie said sharply. "And he shall hear of it from me."

The door beyond them opened and Fannie stepped out into the hall. "Is something amiss?"

"No, nothing," Marie said quickly, "Mr. Hargrave was just on his way to pay his respects to Lady Agatha. He is staying to dinner and we hope Lady Agatha will be able to join us."

"I'm not sure," Fannie began but her words were overridden by Lady Agatha herself who appeared behind Fannie in the doorway, leaning a bit more than usual upon her walking stick.

"I must intrude no longer upon your privacy and kindness," Agatha said. "If a carriage can be seen to—"

"Nonsense," Hero interrupted. "You must stay to dinner."

Lady Agatha smiled in spite of herself. "Hero Hargrave, your manners are deplorable. You cannot issue invitations to other people's tables."

"But we truly want you to join us, Lady Agatha," Marie put in quickly. "Even though"—she smiled impishly at Hero—"I quite agree with you that Mr. Hargrave's manners leave much to be desired."

Delia Dutton did not add to the discussion of Hero Hargrave's lack of manners but the sound that issued from her compressed lips spoke volumes.

"Dear Miss Dutton," Hero said, turning his full attention and his most winning smile on the stern-faced abigail. "Are you feeling quite well?"

She glared at the irrepressible young man and then deliberately ignored him, turning instead towards Lady Agatha. "I hope we may expect the pleasure of your ladyship's company."

"Thank you, Delia. I believe I shall accept Marie's kind invitation. And you, you young scamp," Lady Agatha added, looking towards Hero, "you may offer us a ride home after dinner."

Delia had too much tact to comment upon Lady Agatha's choice of companionship. With set expression she turned away and, head held high, she sailed past the others towards the kitchen stairs.

"I don't think she likes me," Hero said after a moment. Marie and Fannie laughed, Lady Agatha allowing him a small smile.

"You must have done something to get into her bad books," Agatha said.

"He's done a lot more than something," Fannie said and then, seeing her mistress's curiosity directed towards herself, Fannie shrugged. "I imagine," she added weakly.

"Fannie Burns," Agatha said, "you know more than you are saying."

Fannie gave a swift look at Marie, who blushed and looked away. Marie's gaze went towards Hero and then veered away until she found herself staring directly at a very inquisitive Lady Agatha.

"Well?" Lady Agatha asked them all.

Marie swallowed. "It's a rather long story. It began with my nightclothes."

Agatha took a moment to digest this information. "Your nightclothes?" she asked in disbelieving tones.

"I merely brought her home," Hero interjected.

Lady Agatha turned her full attention upon Hero. "In her nightclothes?"

"It was all very innocent," Fannie assured her mistress.

Now Lady Agatha looked truly shocked. "Do you mean to tell me you were a party to such an escapade?"

"Isn't it time to dress for dinner?" Fannie asked.

"Fannie Burns, I want an answer to my question."

"Yes," Marie took a step backwards, "it's time to change. Hero? I mean, Mr. Hargrave," she added hastily when she saw his expression.

"I have nothing to change into," Hero pointed out.

"Oh, dear," Marie fretted, "you'd best not wait alone or Delia is bound to insist you leave."

"I can manage your Delia," Hero said. "At least until you come rescue me."

Will Carston came down the hall towards the small group near the landing, carrying a small pot of coffee on a silver tray. "Good afternoon," Will said with a nod towards Hero and a small bow towards the ladies.

"Is my father awake?" Marie asked.

"He just rang, Miss Marie."

"I've never known him to sleep through the day. I hope he's all right."

"I believe he was up much of the night," Will said.

Fannie ducked her head, her cheeks suddenly rosy.

"Fannie Burns, you are coming with me," Lady Agatha said. "I have more than one question I want answered."

Will Carston let himself into the major's chamber as the ladies departed for their rooms, Hero watching until Marie closed her door without a backwards glance. Then he turned towards the stairs and started down, ready to beard Miss Dutton.

While Daniel Aldworth bathed and dressed for dinner, Lady Agatha allowed Fannie to dress her hair and listened to Fannie's explanations with a deepening frown.

"Young Marie racing out in her nightclothes. I shudder to think what Major Aldworth would think of such goings-on."

"He was there to see it," Fannie said.

Lady Agatha was shocked. "Do you mean to say he *allowed* his daughter to run wild across the grounds and allowed the young Hargrave boy to address her while she was in such undress?"

"He sent her up home and he didn't know Hero was about," Fannie admitted.

"I thought not," Agatha replied.

"But I'm sure Major Aldworth has his own share of secrets," Fannie responded unrepentantly.

Lady Agatha gave her serving-woman a searching look. "What's that you say? Why do you say that?"

Fannie gave an inelegant shrug as she set the last of the ivory pins into her mistress's thick hair. "I think the major would do better to look to his own disposition and bad manners than to worry about his daughter. She has a level head on her shoulders and she's not flighty, even if she is a bit smitten with our Hero and why shouldn't she be?" Fannie demanded. Lady Agatha did not respond. Fannie looked through the mirror and saw her mistress's expression. "Aggie, are you unwell?"

"No," Agatha responded weakly. "I'm fine," she said with a bit more strength. Her face was pale, so bluish that the skin around her eyes looked almost bruised. Her knuckles were white as she grasped the edge of the dressing table, as she willed every fibre in her body to strengthen.

"I'm calling for the doctor," Fannie said.

"No."

"*Yes,* and I won't let you talk me out of it."

"I don't want to intrude on Major Aldworth any further," Agatha said, sounding almost fretful.

"As if you could intrude in Steadford Abbey! I'd like to see the man who could put you out of it, except for that good-for-nothing brother of yours."

"Fannie Burns, you'd best have a care."

"Why? Speaking ill of the dead, is that it? Well, I'd do more than that if I could. I'd spit in his eye, I would, and his being dead hasn't made him one whit better than he was in life. Begging your pardon, but it's the truth," Fannie said and then looked more closely at her employer. Lady Agatha suddenly looked very frail. "Oh, Aggie, what's wrong with you?"

Agatha heard Fannie's heartfelt fear and reached back to pat her abigail's hand. "Nothing but age, Fannie. Nothing but age." She sighed. "We've been together a great many years, we two."

"I came to the kitchens when I was twelve and above-stairs to you when I was sixteen."

"Seventeen seventy-seven." Agatha shuddered. "Do you think I could forget that? As you reminded me recently, that was the year my son ran away." She shivered again.

"You are cold, I'll get your shawl."

"I'm not cold," Lady Agatha said softly but she let her serving-woman retrieve her shawl and place it around her shoulders. If truth be told, she enjoyed Fannie's cosseting, but she hesitated to admit it to the woman who had been servant and friend and confidante and companion for the greater part of both their lives.

"Here you are," Fannie said as she tucked the shawl securely into place.

Agatha sat at the dressing table, staring at its pristine top. "I think you'd best call Timothy and ask him to bring the gig around."

"But you said you'd join them for dinner," Fannie protested.

"I think we'd best leave for home."

"This is your home more than any others who've ever lived in it," Fannie said, her voice rising with her passion. "I say you have more right to be here than all the solicitors and all the bills of sale ever made could ever give anyone else."

"Fannie," Agatha said mildly.

"I don't care what you say, I won't listen. You have a right none others have to the abbey, you're the last Steadford!" Fannie's long-leashed sense of injustice fueled her anger but the passion ebbed away in the face of her mistress's obvious distress. "Aggie? Aggie, what is it?"

"There's no point in discussing what can't be changed," Agatha was saying as someone knocked on the sitting-room door.

Fannie opened the door grim-faced. "Well?"

The major was a little taken aback by Fannie's cold demeanour. "I hope I'm not intruding." He watched her expression change, a hint of a smile coming into his dark and cautious eyes. "I am told we are to have the pleasure of Lady Agatha's company at dinner. I have come to invite you to join us, Fannie Rose Burns."

Lady Agatha came forward, a little surprised by the major's tone and his words. "How kind of you, Major."

"It's not fitting," Fannie said.

"As you have been such a help with the tenant accounts, and as I am sure you normally take your meals with your mistress, I should say it is entirely fitting."

"You are quite right about our habits at home," Agatha replied. "However Fannie was just about to express our regrets, as neither of us can stay. If we could ask that Timothy bring the gig up, we will leave for the gatehouse as soon as possible."

The major looked from the soft-featured and pretty Fannie to the handsome matriarch. "My daughter has been so looking forward to your company at dinner."

"I fear we have presumed upon your kindness for much too long as it is," Lady Agatha replied.

Daniel Aldworth hesitated. "Marie will be disappointed but, of course, if you would rather go, I shall call for the gig."

"Thank you," Agatha responded. "That would be for the best."

The finality in her tone made the major observe her more closely. He tried to read her strange expression. "Best?" he questioned. "Is my hospitality so very distasteful?"

"Of course not. I did not mean to offend."

"Nor have you," Fannie replied sharply. "It is Major Aldworth who is being rude to interrogate you so."

"I meant no disrespect."

Fannie glared at him. "You are making my lady uncomfortable."

The major stared at Fannie briefly, then turned his attention back to Agatha. "I should imagine her discomfort comes from within."

Lady Agatha turned pale as snow as he spoke. Her words, when she found them, were no more than a whisper. "Are you Henry Aldworth's son?"

"I am Sir Henry's heir," Daniel admitted.

Lady Agatha gripped her cane tightly. "I can see him in your eyes. So like—so like—" She faltered and stopped.

"Aggie?" Fannie came near her mistress.

The major raised a quizzical brow, his eyes never leaving Lady Agatha's. "So like whom?" he asked.

"Someone long dead," she said quietly.

Fannie glared at the man. "Major Aldworth, my mistress is in poor health as you well know and this conversation isn't making her any better. Will you please call for the carriage or shall I?"

"I don't understand why our conversation should be detrimental to your lady's health," Daniel persisted.

"Perhaps I truly should explain," Agatha said.

"I would be more interested than you can imagine," the major replied.

"I am calling for the carriage," Fannie announced.

"Wait a bit, Fannie," Agatha said. She saw the major's distrust and continued. "Major, I hope you will forgive us both."

"*He* forgive us!" Fannie objected.

"Fannie, no." Agatha turned her full attention on the tall, scowling man. "She means only to save me distress," Agatha continued. "However after all your kindnesses, I feel I must explain my rather odd behaviour."

Daniel Aldworth's grim visage became even more bleak as he stared at Lady Agatha, waiting for her to continue.

Agatha began to speak, her voice faltering as she tried to explain. "You see, I was acquainted with Sir Henry. He, he was a—a friend. And your likeness to him is uncanny. So that when you first arrived, your name, I thought possibly— in any event, I was proved correct."

She looked up at his unreadable expression, which had grown even darker.

"I fear, madam, you are entirely mistaken," he said coldly.

"I—I beg your pardon?"

"I said, you are mistaken. I am not Sir Henry's son."

"But—you said as much."

"No," came the quick and curt reply. "I said I was Sir Henry's heir and that I am. We met in wartime and he took pity on the unloved boy I once was. He adopted me and left me his entire estate with the provision that I take his name."

"No!" The word escaped Lady Agatha before she could stop it.

Daniel stared at the elegant matriarch. "No?" The word was almost a challenge. "I assure you I am not lying."

Fannie took a step forward. "I think there's been quite enough explanation already."

"Not nearly enough," Daniel corrected. "Lady Agatha obviously feels she knows something more about my origins. Since I can hardly resemble a man I met when I was already fourteen, perhaps we could discuss my resemblance to another?"

"Another?" Fannie questioned.

Agatha was silent, her heart beating furiously, her eyes large with fear.

"Someone else you know?" Daniel asked, angry eyes never leaving the strained and pale woman who did not speak.

"And hasn't she already told you what she thought?" Fannie snapped. "There is no purpose to this nattering on about your looks. I shall go for the gig," she told him.

"You already have said you would," Daniel pointed out.

"I won't leave you alone with her," Fannie told him flatly.

"It's all right," Lady Agatha said quietly.

"Well, you're not and I'll not have this big oaf making you more ill."

"I have no intention of making Lady Agatha ill," Daniel said.

"No?" Fannie turned to face him, her eyes blazing, her hands on her hips. "Then what is it you're intending with all this worrisome talk about people long dead?"

There was a small pause before Daniel spoke again. "Only to tell the truth."

"Well, then, what is it?" Fannie demanded. "What is this truth of yours that's so important you must natter on and on at my lady when she's already weak and ill? You can see she doesn't want to talk about the man, so why will you not just let it be?"

"Fannie—" Agatha remonstrated but her voice was weak and her manner distracted. She said no more.

Daniel Aldworth stared at the angry abigail. "I was not aware Lady Agatha was acquainted with Sir Henry Aldworth. And what I am speaking of has nothing to do with him. But it is an important truth. Especially to Lady Agatha, I should imagine."

Agatha stared at him, her heart in her eyes. "It's you, isn't it? For God's sake, tell me the truth."

"The eyes you see are not Sir Henry's. They are your own."

"What did you say?" Fannie asked, sure her ears were at fault, that she could not have heard his words properly.

"I said I am Daniel Steadford-Smyth."

Silence held the room in thrall, Fannie shocked away from words, Lady Agatha and Daniel staring at each other.

"They sent word, they told us you died aboard the *Victory* . . . with Admiral Keppel. . . ." Her words died away.

"You are crazed," Fannie finally managed to say. Her

voice seemed very far away to Agatha and growing ever
more distant. Lady Agatha sank towards the floor, slipping
over the edge into darkness.

"Aggie!" Fannie and Daniel both reached for her, Daniel's
arms around Lady Agatha before she reached the floor. "Let
go of her," Fannie said but the major paid no heed.

He lifted his mother towards the bed and was crossing
the bedchamber with her in his arms when Sir Harry the
Ghost appeared, materialising straight through the hallway
wall. His transparent body pulsed with anger, his face ferocious as his voice boomed out, shocking the two humans
who heard him.

"What the bloody hell is that?" Daniel asked.

"*What the bloody hell* do you think you're doing with
my Aggie? Release her this instant, you ungrateful whelp,
or so help me, I shall string you up and flay you alive!"

Daniel did not believe his eyes. But his arms felt weak
with shock and he laid Agatha upon the covers as Fannie
realised she had drawn in a breath and forgotten to let it
out. The ghost came towards the bed, and Daniel took a
step back. Fannie quaked in her half-boots but she launched
herself towards the vision, determined to protect Agatha.

"You let my lady alone," Fannie said in a trembling
voice. "She's not to be harmed or you'll answer for it!"

"I? I harm her? Damn and blast you for a fool, woman. But if either of you fools have worried her or hurt
her, *if you've harmed her*"—Sir Harry's threat rose until
it rang in their ears and reverberated around the walls—
"*you'll not live long enough to regret it!*" He gave them
each a withering glance, his eyes blazing like dark coals
in his pale and transparent face. Then he leaned over the
unconscious Lady Agatha. "Aggie—Aggie my love, can
you hear me?"

"Daniel—" Agatha's voice was hoarse. Her eyes flickered open to stare up at Sir Harry's concern. "Harry—
you've never answered when I've called to you . . ."

"I couldn't, love, I don't know why but you could never
truly see nor even hear me."

"Daniel . . . Daniel was here. . . ."

Harry scowled. "Aye, the miserable wretch is here. Boy, come you hither! Why I wasted my time and my fortune on you only to have you use my own blunt to worry my Aggie—"

"Harry—don't." Agatha gazed up at his so long gone, so familiar face. "He doesn't know. Harry, we must tell him."

"Come closer, boy, and let her see you," Harry said, his attention on Agatha.

"I'm here," Daniel said from the opposite side of the bed. He tried to ignore the apparition that sat on the opposite edge of the bed, his ghostly hands reaching for Agatha's thin, blue-veined arm.

"You must be told the truth of it," Agatha said.

"There's no need to talk about my leaving and the whys of it now," her long lost son told her. "I dreamt about this day for years but it no longer seems so very important."

"My lady," Fannie pleaded, even the threat of supernatural terrors unable to stop her. "Please leave off now, you're too tired to wrangle with—with anyone."

"Daniel," Agatha whispered, "you are not Homer Smyth's son. You truly are Harry's son. Mine—and Harry's . . ."

Fannie leaned closer. "Aggie, hush now."

Daniel stared at his mother, his face blank, his mind telling him he had misunderstood. "I beg your pardon?"

"And well you should, upsetting her like this!" Harry said with an angry scowl. "Have you no ears or no wits? Which is it? I never thought a son of mine would be addled in the upper works. Danny, did you never question why I searched you out, why I took such a good-for-nothing young scapegrace under my wing?" Harry looked down at his Aggie. "You never told me, you know, love. But I knew. And I knew that shatter-brained lout you were shackled to had driven Danny from his home so I searched out our young pup."

"Bless me, he's real," Fannie said suddenly, the fact of Harry hitting her shocked brain. She stumbled and Daniel instinctively put out his hand, his arm going around Fannie to steady her.

"Put her down somewhere," Harry told his son. "She's about to have a female fit."

"I am not," Fannie replied with as much spirit as she could muster with her head spinning and her brain telling her she had gone stark raving mad.

"Daniel—" Agatha looked up at the son she had not seen in almost forty years. "I prayed you were alive . . . but they said you were killed at sea . . . at sea . . ." She wanted to say more but she could not keep her thoughts together. Her eyes closed, her breathing shallow, almost indiscernible.

"Aggie!" Harry and Fannie cried out her name in almost the same moment, their fear galvanizing them into action, but Daniel was ahead of them, already reaching for her wrist. He looked up at the ghost of the man he had once known, his sense still not sure of what he was seeing.

"She's breathing," was all he said.

13

THE WINTER OF 1761 was a bleak and cold season, the world drained of all colour. Only white, black and shades of grey remained, white ice clinging to bare black tree branches and stone cottages and the muddy tracks of road that criss-crossed the Dorset countryside. The fields were blanketed with fresh-fallen snow, pristine except for an occasional track of bird or animal or man. Even the sky was a study in greys.

Steadford Abbey sat three storeys tall, its honey-coloured stones looking pale and greyish, its windows glinting wintry in the early morning light. From those windows, if any had looked out so early of a Wednesday morning, Agatha Steadford's eighteen-year-old figure would have been unseen. A grey-cloaked shadow riding a black gelding in the leeward shadows of the abbey hill, she was lost amongst a hundred other shadows.

But she was the only shadow that cried.

Cold winds whipped at her black hair under her grey cape's hood, flicking long tendrils back behind her as she rode as fast as the horse would go. Her streaming tears froze against her wind-reddened cheeks, her heart heavy as she rode towards the abbey spinney.

Within the dark tangle of winter oaks, Harry paced back and forth. His chestnut stallion stood in the snow, watching his master's nervous movements with flicking head and snorting breath.

Harry heard hoofbeats coming near and sprang to the stallion's saddle. Moments later, Agatha entered the woods riding the black gelding, her large eyes brimming with tears.

"Aggie, what have they done to you?"

Agatha shook her head, so relieved to be with her lover she just leaned forward in her saddle to bury her head against his shoulder.

He hugged her close, kissing her forehead. "Sweetest heart, I came as soon as I heard. When I arrived and you weren't here I was afraid they'd caught you out."

"Papa and Nigel roused all the tenants and they've searched all night. I was afraid to come here until they'd passed by. So I ran to the stables and roused Homer and begged him to ride to you with my note. I was so afraid he'd not go to you but tell Papa instead, so I hid outside the stables, just in case I should have to run."

"He's a good lad, your Homer. He said none have a good thing to say for Smyth except your brother Nigel. They say he's wrong-headed and will end up in dun territory if he's not careful. The villagers say if your brother weren't speaking for him, your father would never consider him."

"He's done more than consider him," Agatha told Harry. "He's betrothed me to Smyth and he'll wed me to that odious man the moment he finds me!"

"You will never wed such a one!" Harry promised.

"But what can we do to stop them?"

"We shall run to Gretna Green," Harry told his beloved.

Agatha reached for her lover's hands. "Dearest Harry, we never can. Your father will disown you if you marry a Steadford."

"Steadfords and Aldworths and inheritances be damned." Harry shouted to the windy reaches around them. "I've enough blunt to see us there and wed and once back I shall confront my father and force him to face facts."

"Do you think you can?" Agatha asked.

Harry held Agatha's slim hands tight within his own. "I can if I have you at my side. We love each other, Aggie, and nothing shall ever change that."

They kissed and then he urged her forward in the vague dawning light, the black and the chestnut racing across the countryside, Harry forcing them hard so as to put as great a distance as possible between them and Agatha's pursuers.

Bundled within their cloaks, they raced through the bitter cold of a winter day. They reached the Lion's Head Inn on the Great North Road as a dark grey twilight fell around

them. A crescent moon was already lying low in the sky.
It peeked out from behind the bare branches of the elms
that gave shelter to the ancient inn when they reined in
and handed their horses to an ostler.

Inside the low-ceilinged main room a rotund innkeeper
met the young pair, calling to his daughter and telling her
to show them to the small, snug front bedchamber.

"Our best, it is," the innkeeper's daughter told them,
opening the chamber door.

"It will do," Harry said. He kissed Agatha's forehead
and then turned towards the innkeeper's daughter. "You
may show me to my room," he said.

"Begging your pardon, sir, but this is your room."

Harry could feel Agatha's presence a few feet away. "I
asked for two rooms."

"But we've not got two rooms," the girl responded.

"Then ask someone to move," Harry said.

"Move?" The girl spoke as if she'd never heard the
word.

"I'll pay," Harry said. "Handsomely," he added.

"Harry," Agatha began but he stopped her.

"There must be a room somewhere."

"There is," Agatha said. "Here."

Harry heard the words but they did not fully register until
he turned to face her. "No," he said.

"Yes . . ." she said again, smiling at the man she loved.
She turned towards the innkeeper's daughter and thanked
her, waiting for the girl to go before she turned back to face
her bewildered beloved. "What better way to foil Nigel's
plans?" she asked softly. "Papa can no longer object if
I am already yours. My reputation is lost in any event,
since I have run away with you and we are here, alone,
at night."

Harry grabbed her close. "You are here alone with the
man who will be your husband." He kissed her soundly
before he spoke again. "And none shall ever be able to
keep us apart again."

"None," Agatha vowed, surrendering to his kisses. All
words lost, they fell towards the soft and lumpy bed, their

entire world narrowed to the circle of their arms as they held each other close.

Much later, in the hour just before dawn would break and while Agatha slept, content, in Harry's arms, a hue and cry was raised outside. The noise brought the young lovers awake, Agatha reaching to stop Harry as he sat up and pulled his breeches and boots on.

"Whatever it is, it's not our fight," Agatha told him.

"I'll not leave this room," he promised. He reached for his sword as the noise in the corridor outside became deafening. And then the door to the bedchamber gave way to the marauders.

Agatha screamed, the sound mixing with the yelling voices of the intruders and the slap of steel against steel as Harry attempted to fight off the robbers.

Realising Harry was fighting the robbers alone, Agatha cast about for something, anything, to use as a weapon so that she could help defend them. She reached for the heavy candlestick by the bed, grabbing it with both hands. Rising to her knees on the bed, she smashed it down onto the back of the nearest intruder's head. As the candlestick arced across the room she saw one face near the door clearly.

"Harry!" she shouted as the man she felled slumped to the floor.

Harry turned towards the sound of her voice, a sword grazing his chest as his attention was momentarily distracted. He saw she was alive and turned, thrusting with a vengeance as Agatha's voice rose above the din. "They're Nigel's men!"

Harry heard the words as his sword was already cutting into his attacker's chest.

Agatha's screams grew louder. "Stop! In the name of God, *stop*!"

Light approached in the hallway, a lone lantern and then another bringing narrow beams of light nearer. In the shadowy lantern light the aftermath of the unexpected melee could be seen, the silence broken only by Agatha's sobs as a man lay dying on the bedroom floor.

"Father," she sobbed, on her knees beside the man Harry had felled with his sword.

Ambrose Steadford did not answer. He did not move. Nigel started towards Harry's defenceless back but Agatha saw him and sprang between them. "*No!*" she shouted at her brother.

"He killed our father," Nigel yelled but Agatha outshouted him.

"No, *you* killed our father, you and your avarice and greed and meanness! You brought about this night! If Harry had not defended himself he would lay dead where we slept!"

"You admit it, then, before them all! You are a shameless strumpet!" Nigel bellowed, trying to free himself of his sister's restraining grasp. "You've just admitted your own perfidy!"

"Let her be!" Harry said, coming towards Nigel as his men strained closer.

"Run," Agatha shouted to Harry. "Run before they kill you!"

Harry hesitated. In the shadowy light he could see Nigel's men pushing through the doorway and could hear more coming up the stairs. He knew he could not live out the hour if he stayed. Nigel would take his sister home but he would not physically harm her or allow her to be harmed, that Harry knew. If he lived, he could rescue her from Nigel along the way.

Harry jumped to the wide windowsill and heaved himself out. His last sight was of Agatha sinking to her knees beside her fallen father.

"Aggie, I love you!" he shouted as he jumped.

Nigel called to his men but Agatha shouted louder, calling them back. "No!" she told them all. "Nigel, if you care for anyone other than yourself, if you truly care for our father, you will help me try to heal him and end this farce *now*!"

"Wait," he told the men who followed him. He looked from his sister to his dying father. "I am now the head of the Steadfords," Nigel said. "I give you my word, if you do exactly as I say, I shall call my men off."

Agatha held her bleeding father in her arms, looking up at her brother through tear-blurred eyes. "Our father is not yet dead, Nigel." She crouched over her father, holding him close. "Please, please, father . . . do not die . . . do not die by Harry's sword. . . ."

14

FOR DAYS, SIR HARRY the ghost had hovered near the bed where Lady Agatha lay. Now he watched the tiny movement of her breast as it rose and fell with each breath and counted out the moments until it rose again. Fannie sat staring at her mistress, her reddened eyes and the guttering lamps around her testimony to the lengthening hours as night deepened its shadowy grip.

On the opposite side of the green marble fireplace from Fannie's wing chair Daniel sat in a matching chair, his head thrown back against its dark oriental fabric, his eyes closed. He seemed to be asleep until Lady Agatha stirred, whereupon he sat bolt upright, rubbing his bleary eyes and staring towards the ornate bed.

"Is she all right?" he asked sharply and then, receiving an irritated ghostly glance from Sir Harry, he subsided back into silence and kept his own watch on Lady Agatha as she moved on her pillows.

The half-visible phantom was turned away, his back to the major and Agatha's abigail. The fact that he existed was blow enough to Daniel, but the fact that he was Sir Henry, and his own father, left the major with the uneasy feeling of being in the midst of a dream whilst wide awake.

Daniel stole a glance towards Fannie. The troubled look she cast towards him when she felt his eyes upon her rent his heart. He looked away from her accusing eyes, his brain spinning with a hundred questions that might never be answered.

Across the room Sir Harry leaned over Lady Agatha, his worried face melting into transparency as she stirred and came slowly awake.

"What's happening?" Daniel asked anxiously, starting out of his chair as Sir Harry faded from view.

"God's teeth, don't alarm her!" Sir Harry thundered, his corporeal body fading away.

Distracted, Daniel dragged his fingers through his thick dark hair, his eyes finding Fannie's accusing stare again when he turned back towards the fire. He thought about trying to make her understand what had made him speak to Lady Agatha, understand about the lonely years he had spent with the knowledge that his father disliked him, that his mother never once interceded with his father for Daniel's benefit. Now suddenly, he learned he had been wrong all his life.

The fact that Homer Smyth knew Daniel was another man's son suddenly cast an entirely different light on his history and his mother's reactions. He wanted Fannie to know he had meant no harm to his mother, that he had spoken out of his lifelong pain and could not stop. In the end he knew he did not have the words that could make Fannie understand and so he kept silent on the matter. "I'll be below if I am needed," he said quietly.

"I hardly think you will be," Fannie told him. He stopped at the door and turned as she continued. "Never having the grace to let her know you were alive all these long years, she'd hardly be needing the likes of you now."

Daniel felt guilt rising over the remnants of his hurt and anger. "I wasn't the one who married a cur, nor the one who allowed that loathsome creature to dominate our lives," he said sharply, hurt outweighing guilt.

"And what choice did she have?" Fannie demanded. "You, in your male superiority, you will never understand what it is like for us, how one of our poor gender can be forced to 'choose' what we least want. The choice she had was horrible, and the one that only a male like her odious brother Nigel would thrust upon a poor defenceless female. To be disowned and destitute or to be able to care for herself and her child. With your father dead at your lover's hand, which would *you* in your infinite wisdom choose?"

She glared at the handsome major. "You have no ready answer for that, do you, and now you come back to hurt her and she having given up her freedom and her own peace of mind to ensure you would have a good start in life. What did you do to repay her love? You ran off! Now you deign to come back and you have the effrontery to feel sorry for yourself? It's about time you thought about someone other than yourself, I should say!"

"You can't believe I want her harmed," Daniel said.

"And why can I not?" Fannie demanded.

"If you two fools are going to argue," a ghostly voice intervened, booming out, somehow, within their heads but silent in the room around them, "do it away from my Aggie!"

Chastened, Fannie turned towards her mistress, ignoring the tall man in the doorway. Daniel watched Fannie turn away and then simply left.

He found his daughter sitting in the small blue parlour with Delia. She rose and came towards her father as he approached.

"How is Lady Agatha, Papa?"

Daniel went to the tray of drinks, pouring himself a medicinal measure of port. "She's not awake yet. I've sent for the doctor again."

"Oh, Papa, is she very ill?"

Daniel regarded his daughter for a long moment and then reached to bring her close, holding her as he replied. "I am afraid we do not know, Marie. But I must speak to you, I must tell you."

"Tell me what, Papa?" Marie asked, looking up into her father's distress.

When he did not immediately reply, Delia Dutton stood up. "I'll see to a bit of supper for you, Major," she said.

"I have no appetite," he replied. He sounded very tired.

"All the same, you should at least try to eat," the serving-woman said as she left.

"Papa?" Marie asked when they were alone. "What is it? You must tell me straight, Papa, for I am terribly worried."

Daniel looked deep into his daughter's eyes. "You care about Lady Agatha very much, don't you?"

"Oh, yes, Papa. Very much indeed. She has been so kind and generous, I should hate for anything to happen to her."

Daniel brought his daughter to the sapphire-blue settee and sat with her, keeping her hands within his own. "Marie, I must speak to you."

"Papa, you are frightening me."

He shook his head slowly, trying to allay her fears, but his sober expression did not help ease Marie's worry. "There's nothing to be frightened of," he said. "But there are things you must know, and know now. Before—that is, in case anything should—happen."

"To Lady Agatha?"

"Yes."

"I don't understand," Marie told her father.

"Nor could you," he replied. He took a moment, gathering his thoughts, and then, slowly, began to speak. "Do you remember my telling you of our benefactor? Of the man who befriended me, who died aboard the *Victory*?"

"Sir Henry Aldworth," Marie replied. "You said he was very brave and kind and treated you as a son."

"Yes. I—I don't know how to tell you, other than to say it straight out. I know this will sound as if I am demented, but you must hear me to the end before commenting."

Marie's pale forehead creased into worried lines but she waited and said nothing.

"It seems," Daniel began, "that Sir Henry was, in truth, not only our benefactor. He was my own true father."

Marie's eyes widened. "But, Papa, I don't understand. How could you find this out now? Here? And what has any of this to do with Lady Agatha? And why haven't you told me any of this before now?"

"I did not know Sir Henry was your grandfather."

Marie frowned. "Lady Agatha told you? I've heard there were Aldworths who lived nearby. Did she know them?"

"Yes, she did. And she told me Sir Henry was my father. But he—he—confirmed it."

There was a small pause, Marie trying to make sense of her father's words and finally giving up. "*He* confirmed it," she repeated.

"You needn't look at me thus. He is here. In the abbey."

"Papa, what are you saying?" Marie cried before she

could stop herself. "Sir Henry died when you were a boy."

"Yes, he did." Her father grimaced. "If anyone told me such a story as I am about to tell you, I would send them straight to Bedlam. But I am very afraid that I am not mad, as others have seen him too."

"Papa." Marie leaned forward to kiss her father's cheek and then look earnestly into his troubled eyes. "Papa, you must be very tired. You've barely slept since Lady Agatha fell ill last week."

"Don't think to cosset me into some semblance of sanity. I am telling you the truth."

"Papa, when did Lady Agatha tell you this? And, if Sir Henry were your father, would you not have known it all those years ago? He befriended you. Why did he not tell you?"

"I assume he felt I was too young to understand what had happened. In any event, he did not tell me until now."

"*He* told you now? But you said Lady Agatha told you."

"They both did," Daniel replied.

"But, Papa, that makes no sense, you see? For Lady Agatha to know all this and you just arriving here? And for Sir Henry to be able to speak to you so long after he died."

"It would seem he has been here all along. Waiting."

"But don't you see?" Marie exclaimed, determined to help her father. "How could he have been here, waiting all these years, when you did not even know the abbey existed, let alone that we would end by living here."

"I always planned on coming home," Daniel told his daughter.

"Home?"

"I was born here. In this very house. In the room you have been using."

Marie tried to understand what was happening. Cold fear engulfed her and she held on to her father's hands more tightly than before. "Papa, you and I have been the very best of friends, as well as father and daughter, and you have never told me any of this before. Why would you not have told me of this long ago?"

Daniel spoke gently. "Because I did not know. I am trying to tell you now that there are a great many things more
to life than I have ever given credit to. And that I love
you enough to appear foolish in your eyes at this moment.
Because I want you to know your grandmother while you
still can."

"My grandmother," Marie repeated.

"Yes."

"Papa, we were talking of your father. My grandfather,"
she added although the words made less than no sense.
"Can you not see that you are not being quite sensible?"

"What I can see is that I am saying this all very badly.
Marie, the reason Lady Agatha told me about Sir Henry—
the reason she knew he was my father—was because she
knew better than any who my father was. She knew it was
not Homer Smyth because she is my mother." Once he had
said the words he felt a great wave of relief. He continued
in a stronger voice. "She is your grandmother and I should
have told you so long since."

Marie clung to her father. "Papa, you are saying so many
things and all of them at odds with sense. I don't understand
any of this."

"Marie, you must understand, for your grandmother is
not well. I was born here. Lady Agatha is my mother. Your
grandmother. I should have told you that long since but I
felt I had reason not to. That I was not wanted here and
therefore my child would not be wanted either. I wanted
you to enjoy your birthright, your inheritance, without having to know of the acrimony and bitterness in the past. What
I did not know, until this very day, was that I was wrong in
some of my assumptions. And wrong in keeping you from
knowledge of your grandmother." He hesitated. "Nor did I
know that Sir Henry was my father."

"Papa—" Marie said again and then stopped, staring at
her father's unhappy face. "I'm sorry. Please continue."

Daniel Aldworth's moody eyes met his daughter's appre-
hensive gaze. "It is I who should apologise, not you. It
seems my meeting Sir Henry was not by chance all those
years ago. He sought me out. Marie, please understand the

man whom I thought to be my father—Homer Smyth—was a dastardly fool. I was ashamed of him and ran from him and never wanted to come back to Dorset while he was alive, never wanted to speak of him to you. And so I spoke little of my family. Our family. I felt they had never wanted me and therefore neither I nor mine should ever want them. But I was wrong."

"But Papa—"

"Please hear me out," Daniel continued. "I was born Daniel Steadford-Smyth and I thought myself to be Homer Smyth's son for all my life until this day. I was ashamed that I was his son and I was ashamed of my feelings."

It took Marie a moment to put his words together. "You were born—Daniel Steadford-Smyth. That was your name before you inherited Sir Henry's estate?"

"Yes."

"But then you *knew* that Lady Agatha was related to you before we came here."

Daniel held his daughter's hands. "Lady Agatha is my mother and, yes, I knew that before we came. I have been remiss in not telling you so long before now."

He saw Marie's surprise slowly turn to realisation, her dark eyes never leaving his. "You bought the abbey because of her," she said.

"No. I bought it because of us. And that's not entirely true, either. Yes, I wanted to come back triumphant, I wanted your grandmother to see how well I had done, despite her lack of interest or love. And now I find she had neither lack of interest nor of love."

"Papa, forgive me, but you are not making sense. You say you were born a Steadford-Smyth, that Lady Agatha is my grandmother. But then you say Sir Henry Aldworth is your father."

"Lady Agatha was to marry Sir Henry but was prevented by her family and forced to marry her brother's boon companion, Homer Smyth."

"What you are saying is—" Marie could not voice the words.

"Yes," he said quietly. "I am telling you what transpired

long before either of us were born."

"But—how could she tell you all this whilst she is so ill?"

"I know this will sound so daft you will think me touched in the head but most of this he told me. Your grandfather. Marie, don't look so strangely at me, Sir Henry *is* here." He saw his daughter's expression and continued. "He has stayed by her side through all these years."

"Papa," Marie said gently, "you told me he died long ago."

"And so he did."

Marie digested her father's words. "And so he did," she repeated.

Daniel stood up, running his hand through his hair, his distracted expression worrying his only child. "He died many years ago and left all to me and mine. But he came back here, in some way I do not understand, and he has stayed close to Lady—to my mother—your grandmother— ever since." He saw his daughter's strange expression and blurted out the truth. "He is a ghost!" Daniel fairly shouted. He waited for his daughter to accuse him of madness.

"A ghost," Marie repeated.

"Call me mad," Daniel said.

"Sir Harry."

Daniel stared at his daughter. "I beg your pardon?"

"Sir Harry the Ghost," Marie repeated. "Hero and I, I mean Mr. Hargrave and I, we've seen him. We have seen Sir Harry, at any rate."

Dumbfounded, her father stared at her. "I think we are all going quite, quite mad," he finally informed Marie.

When the doctor arrived, Marie was left alone with her thoughts, her father going above to hear the doctor's prognosis.

Soon thereafter, while Marie attempted to make sense of all that was happening, Hero Hargrave arrived at the abbey to ask after Lady Agatha. From the top of the staircase, Major Aldworth heard the young man's voice and called down to the entrance hall.

"The doctor is with her ladyship now. Please come up, I must speak to you about my daughter."

"Sir?" Hero replied as he joined the major in the Long Gallery.

"It is possible that you may no longer wish to call upon my daughter," Major Aldworth said as he paced the Long Gallery, the serious expressions of generations of Steadfords standing silent witness as he explained.

Hero's face was a study in disbelief by the time Daniel finished speaking. "Oh, I do say, Major, I mean, upon my word, Lady A? I can hardly credit it."

Daniel stiffened. "Therefore you can see why it may be impossible to continue your addresses to my daughter."

Hero looked blank. "I beg your pardon, sir? I don't quite follow."

"I have told you of our past."

"Yes, Major, and I must say I can hardly believe Lady Agatha was ever that—that—*young*—but I must assume you have the right of it. But what does that have to do with Marie and me, sir?"

Daniel stared at the younger man. "I hardly think it should be necessary for me to draw pictures for you. The circumstances of my birth are most unusual, beyond the pale of polite society. I will not have my daughter suffer because of this and must therefore ask, if you truly care about her welfare, that you not allow her to be subjected to such a fate."

"Sir, I would never allow anyone to cast aspersions upon Marie."

"Then you must see why there is no future for the two of you. You can hardly fail to inform your family, and I am sure they will find Marie ineligible for your considerations."

"Begging your pardon, Major, but you have been gone from our shores a very great while indeed. Why half of London's polite society hardly knows whose child is whose these days, except for the first, the heir, of course. Deuced bad luck for you, sir, if you'll pardon me for saying so, but then, all's well that end's well, what?"

"I beg your pardon?" Daniel said, his tone frosty.

"Well, sir, it's all turned out in the end, what? I mean, you're home and know the right of it all. Of course, Sir Harry would have been roasted alive in the old days, devilish bad *ton* to seduce innocent young girls, supposed to wait until they've married and done their family duty and produced an heir before seducing the gorgeous creatures."

"You seem to know a great deal too much about the rules of seduction," Marie's father told Hero.

Hero smiled. "More than I care to, sir, and it's a dashed boring game, I can tell you that. I've a mind to settle down and make your daughter an exemplary husband, if she'll have me. And, of course, if you approve, sir," Hero added quickly.

Daniel stared at Hero. "It strikes me that not the least part of my amazement at your response is your lack of surprise over my story of a ghost."

Hero had the grace to look a bit guilty.

"I can see that you are most anxious to explain," Daniel said dryly.

"Well, sir, it's just that I have some little knowledge of the abbey ghost."

"Yes?" Daniel persisted.

"You see, we've, that is I've, seen him."

"We?" The one word had sharp edges.

"Actually, Marie and I. Sir." Hero smiled.

Daniel did not. "And?" he prompted.

Hero began, slowly, to explain their meeting with the ghost of Sir Harry, Daniel staring at him more and more intently. When Hero was done, Daniel was silent.

"Sir?"

Daniel shook his head. "I am a military man. I am trained to believe only in the logical and ghosts are not logical."

"But, forgive me, sir, are you not also trained to believe the experience of your own eyes?"

"That I am," Daniel said and then sighed. "And how am I to reconcile the two, I have no idea."

15

LADY AGATHA SLOWLY gained strength throughout the following days, but Daniel was still unable to sleep soundly, rising to check on her again and again. And so it was a haggard-looking Major Aldworth who greeted the arrival of his niece and her family late of a Thursday night. The abbey entrance hall was a chaotic scene as the Duke and Duchess of Melton arrived with three sleepy children, two tired maids and the redoubtable Pickering, who oversaw the removal of trunks and boxes from the two hired coaches which were drawn up to the portico.

Oil lamps flared light out upon the driveway stones as Jane came through the doorway, her son racing ahead towards the stairs. Jane called to her husband to disengage their young son from the newel post, grabbed their toddler, young Agatha, before she followed her brother and thrust the girl towards the nursemaid before reaching to check on the newest babe who slept in his nurse's arms.

"I can't imagine how he can possibly sleep through all this," Jane declared as she adjusted her baby's blanket.

"Perhaps it's the hour, Your Grace," the major said from the head of the stairs.

"Yes, I'm sure you are quite right." Jane turned to face the tall, dark man who came down the stairs. "But still it is a wonder."

"I quite agree," her host responded.

"You must be Major Aldworth, and we must beg your pardon. You are Major Aldworth?" she questioned, her eyebrows rising, her other thoughts forgotten as she gave the handsome major a much longer and more searching look. "Aldworth. That's very strange. Are you possibly any relation to Sir Henry Aldworth?" she asked.

"I seem to be his son," Daniel said stiffly.

Jane's eyes widened. "Oh, I do say, how capital for you! Seem to be?" she added.

"I beg your pardon?"

"I don't mean to pry, it's just your phrasing was—well— in any event, have you seen him since you arrived?" Jane questioned and then broke into merry peals of laughter at Daniel's expression. "Oh, I know he's supposed to be dead, lo, these many years, but you must have seen him since you arrived. Charles," she called to her husband, "come and tell the major I am not completely off in the upper works, will you?"

Charles Edward Graham, fourth Duke of Melton, came forward. "I can hardly lie, pet," he said to his wife before he bowed to his host. "My wife is much more sane than she at first appears, Major. And I hope you will forgive us this arrival at such an ungodly hour. We are doubly indebted to you for letting us descend upon you in such a fashion and at such an hour. I assure you, we will not be staying longer than to let her ladyship know we have arrived. I understand she's feeling poorly and has kept to her bed these past weeks?"

"Yes," Jane said. "Homer has us quite worried, Major. He did not know precisely what was wrong. We had promised to come for her birthday."

"She collapsed and the doctor feared it was her heart but she is much improved. You are welcome, as she is, to stay as long as you wish," Daniel said. "I have hopes that she will consider staying permanently." Daniel eyed Jane intently. "Forgive me, but you spoke of seeing Sir Henry."

"He told us to call him Sir Harry," Jane offered and when she saw Daniel's stricken expression, she smiled. "I'm sure you think me demented."

"I am fast becoming certain dementia may be a family trait," Daniel replied. "Since my daughter's reaction was as prosaic as yours, there are three of us who are obviously losing our wits."

"Actually, you'd best count me in for a fourth since I've seen him too," Charles put in. "And I assure you I thought I had gone stark raving mad when first I did. But he seems to take quite an interest in young lovers." Charles smiled at his wife. "Is he why you are here?" Charles asked innocently.

"I beg your pardon?" Daniel replied. "Why should he be?"

"Nothing. I just thought, well, it's a strange coincidence. You being an Aldworth and buying the abbey and all."

Daniel hesitated. "There is no coincidence," he told Jane and her husband. "I was born here."

"Born here?" Jane questioned.

"My father was Sir Henry but I was born Daniel Steadford-Smyth."

"Why, but that's my maiden—" Jane stopped in midsentence. *"Daniel?"* she asked again, her eyes growing large. *"My Uncle Daniel?"*

Daniel gave a stiff little bow. "I believe I am your uncle."

"Good grief," Charles said into the ensuing silence. "What has been transpiring since we've been away in America?"

"But we were told you had died long before I was born!"

"I was reported dead in the war," Daniel replied. "Obviously the report was a bit premature."

Jane stared at him. "But you never came home, never wrote to let Gram know you were still alive."

"I did not think any wished to hear from me. Least of all my mother."

"I don't understand," Charles put in.

"It is a very long story," Daniel responded.

"Yes," Jane said, "it must be. And I should like to hear all of it. But first I should very much like to see Grandmother."

"Let me show you the way," Daniel said.

Jane turned to her husband, who kissed her brow and promised to see to the children until she returned.

"But she'll want to see you," Jane protested.

"There will be plenty of time," Charles promised. "Plenty of time after we are settled at Stoneybridge," he repeated.

"Stoneybridge?" Daniel interjected.

"There are no suitable accommodations in Wooster so we have taken rooms in Stoneybridge and shall repair there immediately after seeing Lady Agatha," Charles said.

"But you can't stay so far away," Daniel responded. "That is to say, you must, of course, stay here."

"I assure you, Major, we have no intention of imposing ourselves in such a fashion."

"Nor shall you," Daniel said. "There is room enough for a score of visitors and more and I am being quite selfish in asking you to stay. I am convinced Lady Agatha shall be much better far sooner if you are here to cheer her, Your Grace. And we are family, finally, in one way or another."

Jane reached to press Daniel's arm. "Uncle Daniel has the right of it, Charles, dear," Jane declared, and kissed her husband's cheek. "What a strange feeling, to be able to say Uncle Daniel. I must say it is a pleasure I never thought to have." She gave Daniel another winning smile before turning back towards her husband. "Charles, you must tell Pickering to see to our brood and come up as soon as you can."

"Yes, dearest," Charles said as he let his wife go and watched her walk forward with her newfound uncle and begin to ascend the wide staircase. "I must say it seems you always get your own way," he called out.

Jane flashed him a brilliant smile. "Yes, I always do. You see, I married the most indulgent and handsomest of husbands!" So saying, she linked her arm with Daniel's and disappeared up the broad stairs.

"Mama, Mama," young Agatha called out. She toddled towards the stairs but her father scooped her up into his arms.

"Come along and help me, you scamp. Charlie," he called to his elder son, "run and get Pickering."

"May I be of help?" a voice asked from behind the duke as his young son ran out across the wide portico. The duke turned to see Delia Dutton offering her services. "I am Dutton, Your Grace."

Pickering came through the door just in time to hear the serving-woman's words. Laden with packages, he unceremoniously dumped them into her arms. "Thank you," he responded in frosty accents. "We are only unloading packages we have brought for Lady Agatha and Miss Burns. If you will follow me," he continued, waiting for her and then sending the duke a look over the woman's head. "Please give our best to Lady Agatha, Your Grace," he said pointedly. "I shall carry on here."

Charles grinned. "Are you giving me my marching orders, Pickering? I think you're getting above yourself these days."

"Yes, sir," Pickering replied, not in the least disturbed by his employer's rebuke. "This way, please," he said to Delia.

Delia Dutton, laden with packages, followed the tall and dour-looking servant, her mouth set into disapproving lines. "I shall show *you* where to place them," she said sharply.

While Delia Dutton argued with the duke's man, upstairs Jane tiptoed into Lady Agatha's bedchamber, Daniel coming behind.

Jane's eyes strained across the darkness to where her grandmother lay on the bed, a small oil lamp on the table beside her. Fannie looked up and then stood, her face wreathing in smiles even as tears sprang to her eyes. She reached for Jane and hugged her close.

"I can't believe you're finally home. You're just what she needs, you'll make her right as rain," Fannie said.

"How is she?" Jane asked.

"She's resting comfortably."

"Should we wake her?" Jane asked.

"Fannie?" Agatha asked. She opened her eyes and looked across the gloomy room. "Fannie, it was so strange . . . I thought I heard Jane—"

"You did, Grandmama," Jane said as she came closer to Lady Agatha's bed. The lamp cast a soft glow over her face as she leaned down to kiss Lady Agatha's cheek. "I've come home, dear Gram, and I've brought Charles and little Charles and your namesake and our littlest one." Jane stopped her rush of words and kissed her grandmother's forehead. "He was named in honour of my uncle whom I never thought to see and who is standing here beside us. We love you so much, Grandmother."

Agatha turned towards Jane's voice, her dark eyes fighting to focus and then, suddenly, she smiled. "My Jane, my little Jane, you're home . . . ? Did you see Daniel?"

"Yes, and I think he is very handsome, Grandmama."

Fannie made a face at Jane's words but said nothing more than to ask if anyone wanted tea.

"My Daniel . . ." Agatha said softly.

"I am here," he said quietly, earning a startled look from Fannie. He leaned closer to his mother and reached for her hand. "What do you need?"

Jane straightened. "I shall give you some privacy. In any event we are parched through, and I for one shall faint dead away if I can't have a bit of tea and a bite of something before we continue to our lodgings."

"Continue?" Fannie asked, affronted. Her accusing gaze went towards Daniel.

He shrugged and spread his hands wide. "I have told them they must stay."

"Yes, well, tell them again," Fannie said. "I'll just go see to the tea." She wiped her tears with her apron.

Agatha held on to Jane's hand, staring up into her sky-blue eyes, drinking in the sight of her granddaughter. "It's been so long," she said.

"Too long," Jane was saying as Fannie left the room.

Daniel followed Fannie out into the hall. "She seems to be a bit better."

"No thanks to you," Fannie said sharply, putting her back to him.

Daniel reached out for Fannie's arms, spinning her around to face him, his expression grim. "This isn't my fault. I asked them to stay."

"Then make them know they're not only welcome, they're needed. You owe her that, since you've certainly done her no favour keeping after her about the past when there's naught to be done about what's already done. Let go of my arm," she insisted.

"No."

Fannie stared up into Daniel's dark and unreadable gaze, startled. "What did you say?"

Daniel's voice lowered. "I said no."

Fannie faltered, her heart giving the strangest lurches. "I don't understand," she said faintly.

Daniel stared down into Fannie's honest blue eyes. Her arms felt pleasantly round and warm in his grip. He could hear the catch in her voice, her breath coming in shallow gasps as she watched him, half-afraid, half-curious.

"Perhaps you don't understand," he told her, his eyes and his words suddenly moody. He released his grip.

For one split second, Fannie stood where she was. Then she pulled back as if burned, suddenly afraid of being too near him. She sped towards the door to the servants' stairs, never looking back to see the man who watched her from under hooded eyes.

Daniel was lost in thought when the duke came up the stairs towards him, Pickering in the lead, closely followed by Delia Dutton.

"I'll show you to the spare rooms, where you can have the women change the children," Delia was saying, hard pressed to keep up.

"My memory is an entirely sufficient guide," Pickering told the woman. "Having had a *much* longer association with the abbey than you have, Miss Dutton, I am sure you are needed elsewhere. You *are* Miss Aldworth's abigail, I believe?"

"Yes."

"Then you needn't worry yourself about household duties better left to those who are used to assuming such burdens."

Major Aldworth came down the hall towards the duke. "Major Aldworth," Charles said, "I beg your pardon. Perhaps I should call you Steadford?"

"Aldworth is my legal name," Daniel replied.

"Major Aldworth, are you quite sure you wish a brood

such as ours to descend upon you willy-nilly? I mean, here you've barely learnt you have a family and we descend upon you *en masse*. And we do, after all, have perfectly adequate lodgings waiting, since we assumed Lady Agatha would be ensconced in the gatehouse. There's no need for you to go to the extra bother."

"It will be good for her to have you here," Daniel said. "And for Marie," he added after a moment.

"I tried to give Lady A back the bloody abbey before we left, did she tell you?" Charles asked.

"No," Daniel replied. "But we have had little chance for conversation."

"Yes, well, I knew Nigel Steadford for a wrong 'un from the first glance I had of him. Sorry, I realize he was your uncle, and it's best not to speak ill of the dead, but the truth is the truth."

"I barely knew him," Daniel responded. "And even as a child I didn't like him."

"You showed good taste. In any event, he had taken the abbey away from Lady A, by hook and by crook thanks to that gambler Homer Smyth, and when we left I tried to give it back to her but she'd have none of it. She is a stickler for what's right and proper."

"It would seem so," Daniel answered noncommittally.

Charles realised the effect his words must be having on Agatha's long lost son and reddened. "Sorry, old man."

"Don't be."

Jane called to her husband from the doorway to Lady Agatha's chambers, asking him to come and bid her hello. "Have you done all this?" she asked Daniel as Charles deposited their youngest child in his nurse's arms and came forward.

"I beg your pardon?" Daniel asked.

"This." Jane waved her hand. "All of it. The abbey is simply beautiful. Except, I must say, for all the oriental splendour in my grandmother's rooms. That's a bit much but I can see someone's spent a fortune on the old house. We had the most awful worn-out drugget along the hall here and drafts from chinks and cracks around the windows and everything was going to wrack and ruin. You have done wonders," she said as Charles disappeared past her into her grandmother's chambers.

"It is not my doing," Daniel replied. "For good or for ill, we've been here only a few months and most of what you see was done by the former owner, a merchant by the name of George Beal."

"Well, someone has done wonders. Except for Gram's rooms."

"You'd best ask your grandmother."

Jane gave her uncle a very questioning look. "What a strange way to refer to your own mother."

Daniel looked down and then, resolutely, looked up to meet his niece's gaze. "I suppose it is, but then I have only just found out a great many things."

Jane reached for Daniel's arm. "It must be very painful for you, coming home after all these years and so much changed."

"Home . . ."

"You must tell me about your life abroad. And about your wife and my mother and everything."

"I never saw your mother again after I left."

"Ah, but at least you knew her. I never did," Jane said wistfully.

"I don't know what I can tell you," he replied.

"Anything you remember. Everything you remember," Jane amended. Impulsively, she reached up to kiss her uncle's cheek.

Daniel was both surprised and touched. The hint of a tentative smile glinted deep in his eyes. "I shall try," he promised.

"Good," she pronounced. "And we shall tell you stories of your father."

"I beg your pardon?"

"Well, you said you've seen him too."

"Yes . . . it would seem I have," he said, his brain still telling him he should disbelieve the proof of his own senses.

"Wonderful," Jane said. She smiled wide. "I wonder where he is that he hasn't said hello to us yet. Did you know if it weren't for Sir Harry, Charles and I would never have married?"

"No, I did not," Daniel said, obviously uncomfortable with the turn of conversation. "You seem to take its—his—presence—very much in stride."

"Of course. I was the first to see him, you see. Except for the odd maid or two who must have upset him awfully because he scared them half out of their wits. We had some who ran screaming from the house."

"I can well believe," Daniel said dryly.

"But you see Charles and I are beholden to your father and, as I say, I was the first to actually talk to him. He was quite put out at having been so long alone. But even before that I was positive there was something Gram was not telling me from the moment she nearly fainted when I wore her red ball gown."

"I beg your pardon?"

"It's a long story," Jane told Daniel. "We shall have time to tell each other everything." She reached to hug him. "I'm so glad I have an uncle! I've never had any family to care for but Grandmama." Another thought occurred, making her large eyes round with surprise. "Since you are my uncle and Sir Harry is your father, then Sir Harry is my great-uncle, by marriage, is he not?"

"Not precisely," Daniel answered.

"Yes, but the same as, is he not? Oh, this is wonderful. Just imagine, I have a relation who is a ghost!"

"Your Grace?" One of the nursemaids, hearing the sound of her mistress's voice, appeared at a doorway across the hall. "Is there anything you need?"

"No, thank you, Emily," Jane replied. "Are the children asleep?"

"Not yet, Your Grace, although well they should be."

"They're probably overtired," Jane replied. She smiled at Daniel. "I shall see to the children and then, if we may, Charles and I shall keep Grandmama company until she falls asleep. This is so good of you, letting us all stay for her birthday. Are you inviting Elizabeth and Giles to stay too?"

"Elizabeth and Giles?"

"Yes, Giles Steadford must be your second cousin or something very like. They are coming for Grandmama's birthday too. I warn you, they have two children younger than our Charles and Agatha. You shall be up to your elbows in children if you say you want us all to stay."

Daniel's smile was wistful. "I always thought the abbey should be full of children."

"So did I," Jane replied, smiling back at him. "As if one big happy family lived here."

"Yes," Daniel replied slowly. "As if."

"This is going to be so much fun," Jane declared. And then, linking arms with her uncle, she started towards her grandmother's room, chatting about life in America.

Early the next morning, Marie was up and out to the spinney where she huddled against the huge gnarled trunk of an ancient oak. Her slim figure was engulfed by a great dark cloak that blended into the shadows. Hero was already reining in his horse before he saw her.

"I came as quickly as I could," he said as he leapt off his horse and came near enough to see the glistening tears that had spilled down her cheeks.

"What's all this?"

"We must not see each other again. You must leave me this instant," she told him, her voice forlorn.

"Stuff and nonsense," Hero responded.

"You don't understand," she began but he stopped her with a kiss and then held her close.

"I understand everything I must. Which is that we love each other and you will be my wife."

"I cannot. That is why I sent for you. To tell you. I cannot."

"You can and you will and I won't hear of anything less if I have to drag you to Gretna Green!"

"You never would!"

"I would and I will, if you haven't more sense than to run scared at a bit of a turn up. I wondered why you've been avoiding me."

"I have learned my father is a—a love child! I shall never marry, nor would your parents allow us to marry, and well you know it!"

"My parents may try to talk *you* out of it," Hero told her. "Once they know you, they'll love you and worry about saddling you with the likes of me, but I shall tell them to stop and I shall insist you pay them no mind and we shall say our 'I do's' and that will be that. As to your letter, I know all about it. He told me himself."

"He never did!"

"He did and if the whole world said nay, I'd still have you to wife, my dearest, most adorable, Marie Aldworth. But you need not fear for none shall say us nay. Dear heart, you have led a very sheltered life if you think the facts of your father's birth will in some way make you ineligible in this day and age."

"You don't understand! My grandfather is a ghost!"

"Well, after all, he wasn't always one," Hero said encouragingly. "And he seems to like me well enough, so why should that bother us?"

"You are very sure of yourself, Mr. Hargrave."

"Yes," he said happily. "I am." He said no more, his lips searching out hers as she gave in to her feelings and kissed him back with all her heart.

"Miss Marie!" Delia Dutton's voice rang out from behind the young couple. "I saw you sneak away from the house!"

Startled, Marie drew back from Hero's embrace but his arms were still around her as she faced her abigail. "Yes?"

"Yes? Is that all you have to say for yourself?" Delia demanded. "Mr. Hargrave, unhand my charge!"

"Hardly likely," Hero replied. "You are speaking of my betrothed."

"Your—what?" Delia asked, startled.

"My intended," Hero repeated. He offered his arm to Marie. "Shall we tell the others?" he asked as they started back up the hill towards the huge stone house that crowned the summit.

16

OVER THE NEXT few weeks, as Lady Agatha grew in strength, Daniel awoke each morning to find the abbey alive with the sounds of children and the rushing about of servants' feet. Doors opened and closed in the distance, the nursemaids' voices called out in loud whispers and young voices carolled back their replies. It all seemed strange in the usually silent abbey and yet strangely comforting.

He lay within the warmth of his bedclothes, watching the November sun cast changing patterns out beyond his windows. Something made him look towards his fireplace and, in front of it, Sir Harry stood staring down at the cold embers of last night's fire.

"Is she all right?" Daniel asked, feeling foolish even as he spoke.

Sir Harry turned at the sound of his son's voice. "Aye, she's doing better. In all events she's awake and eating a bit more."

"Good." Daniel watched the ghostly figure. "Why did you never tell me the truth?"

"I always tell the truth," Harry replied a bit self-righteously.

"You never told me you were my father all those years ago before you—" Daniel searched for a suitable word—died did not seem appropriate since Henry Aldworth was apparently no more dead than he was alive.

Harry sighed, his broad shoulders rising and falling in their tattered purple velvet. "I never lied to you. I simply didn't tell you the why of it. It was not my truth to tell," he said unhappily.

Daniel sat up, throwing his covers off and reaching for his robe. "Will?" He called out for his servant who slept in the next room and then he looked back at the ghost. "I owe all that I have to you, but I am finding it deuced hard to reconcile myself to this situation."

"You mean to my being your father or my being a ghost?"

"Both," Daniel replied.

Sir Harry looked glum. "I can hardly blame you."

"Why did you not marry her?"

"I couldn't. I killed her father."

"What!"

"You don't have to shout," Harry told his son in aggrieved tones. "I didn't do it on purpose. I didn't even know it was him. We were on our way to Gretna Green, to be married before that slippery brother of hers got old Ambrose to force her marriage to Homer Smyth. I thought we were beset by robbers. When we realised who our attackers were, it was too late and I had to flee. Nigel told her I'd been caught and killed and forced her to wed that good-for-nothing Smyth. Smyth wanted her inheritance and he got it, for what good it did him. In the end Nigel got it all, which was his purpose all along and both of them died unmourned."

"She never told me any of this," Daniel said. "I thought my father—Smyth—hated me and I him. I ran off and kept on running because of it."

"And when did you give her the chance to tell you?" Harry argued. "It's not the sort of thing you tell a young boy, now, is it? You were just turning fourteen when you ran off to the army. Why didn't you come back long since to see her?"

"You must have been startled to see me arrive here at the abbey," Daniel said.

Harry gave his son a long, sad, look. "Aye, that I was. And afraid for your mother."

"Why afraid?"

"Because any could see you felt ill used when you thought she didn't recognise you right away."

"She showed not one sign of recognition."

"Ah, but she did, lad. You just didn't see it, because she didn't want you to. She saw herself in you and, aye, she saw a bit of me too. But she knew you were long dead and she didn't want to seem foolish in front of a stranger. And a stranger is what you were—what you are until you make peace with her."

Daniel hesitated. "Is it too late?" he asked finally, searching the ghostly features across the room as he tried to make sense of what was happening.

"Too late for what? To let her know you care? To tell her you understand? That you feel no blame towards her? You've lived your life knowing she was here and never coming near. She thought you dead or she'd have scoured the earth to find you. You may not need her love, Daniel, but she needs your forgiveness more than she's ever needed anyone or anything."

Daniel stared at the ghost, who began to fade through the wall as Will Carston came through the door from the next room. Will carried a tray of morning tea and he brought the news that new arrivals were at that very moment depositing baggage and children in the entry hall.

"I believe the names are Sir Giles and Lady Elizabeth Steadford, sir. It would seem you have a distant cousin."

"I seem to be growing quite a large family tree."

"It's good to have family around one," Will said. "And it would seem you have a great deal more family than we ever imagined." His curious expression told Daniel that the servants were already aware of his kinship to Lady Agatha. "Did you know, sir? I mean, when you bought the abbey and all, did you know your family was here?"

Daniel's expression clouded. "I knew my—my mother"—he stumbled over the unfamiliar word—"was still alive through the solicitors who made arrangements for the keys to be held for our arrival. I had rather imagined my sister would also be here, along with a crowd of brats."

"Ah, then you didn't know your mother had been so long alone."

"No," Daniel replied moodily.

"Well, none's alone now, sir," Will said in a bracing tone. "There's niece and cousin and all their families to be seen to."

"And mother and father."

"And—I beg your pardon, sir? Did you say father?"

Daniel roused himself and turned to search his valet's questioning face. He gave Will a wry smile. "Don't tell me they've not spoken to you of the abbey ghost. It would seem the gossip mill has been rife with all else."

Will watched his employer. "Are you sure you're feeling quite well, Major?"

"Under the circumstances, I should say I am feeling as well as anyone possibly could when suddenly coping with an ill mother, a ghost for a father and a seemingly never-ending arrival of nieces, cousins and what not."

"A ghost, Major?"

"I can't imagine how you've missed him," Daniel said.

"Are you gammoning me, sir?"

"Truthfully, Will, I'm not sure precisely what I am doing at this juncture."

"Well, sir," the valet answered quietly. "It's rather a great deal to take in, all at once, as it were."

"It's a great deal more than you realise," Daniel said before he left to check on Lady Agatha.

Downstairs, Jane was hugging Elizabeth and being introduced to her youngest cousins. "Grandmama's letters were so full of you, I felt as if we were fast friends even before you came to visit us in America the year before last."

"Yes and what a journey that was. I still sometimes can feel the pitch and toss of the ship. Do you know I had our Agatha on the voyage home?"

"Yes and now she has a baby brother."

Elizabeth laughed as she reached to take him from his nurse. "Giles said that was terribly efficient of me but I told him I have no intention of continuing to give Becky— we call our Agatha Becky, from her middle name—in any event, I have no intention of giving her further brothers or sisters for a good long time."

Fannie was hugging young Becky. She released her and greeted Elizabeth before showing the nurse up the stairs to the rooms that would be theirs.

Jane linked arms with Elizabeth and followed the other women. "I was wondering how we should all tell our

Agathas apart," she said, laughing. "Come along and have a bit of tea while you recover from your journey."

Sir Giles Steadford called out to his wife from below. "Elizabeth, how is she?" he asked as he came towards them.

"I was just about to ask," Elizabeth told her husband and looked back towards Jane. "Young Tim said Lady Agatha was feeling poorly and has been bedridden here."

"That's not all he said," Giles added. "We've been told the strangest thing, Jane."

Jane grinned. "About the ghost or about my uncle?"

"The ghost!" Giles exclaimed. "You mean, you've seen him?"

Jane's eyes lighted. "He's still here and you'll never guess who he really is! I've got all kinds of things to tell you both but first you must revive from your journey. Grandmama has been a bit weak but I think it's just with the surprise of—of everything which I shall tell you as soon as you've had a chance to get your wits about you."

"She's not in danger, then," Elizabeth asked.

"She's not quite all the thing, but once you've seen her you will be able to tell us much better than we could tell you since you are the former nurse amongst us."

"Jane, what do you mean about who our ghost really is?" Giles persisted. "He's Sir Harry Aldworth, isn't he?"

"Yes," Jane agreed, smiling happily, "he's that too. And I'm simply bursting to tell you more but I know Grandmama is awake and just pining to see you, so hurry off and change. As soon as you're ready we can slip in to see her and we'll even feed you breakfast, how does that sound?"

"Wonderful," Giles proclaimed from the stairs above them. "Travelling makes me ravenous."

"It must be a family trait," Jane replied. "Here you are," she told them as they reached the room. Delia and Fannie were both inside with Marie, the two children and the nurse. Giles took one look at the chaos and groaned.

"Marie," Jane called, "come and meet your relatives. Don't, for pity's sake, ask me which degree of relation

you are to them. Giles and Elizabeth, this is my cousin
Marie Aldworth."

In the middle of the noisy upstairs sitting-room a young
baby cried, little Becky tried to get her father's attention,
the nurse tried to calm both children and Giles Steadford
stared at the lovely young Marie.

"Aldworth?" he questioned, his brow rising.

"I told you there was much to talk of," Jane said, grinning.
"Now *do* hurry."

"We shall," Elizabeth promised, her curiosity near to
spilling over.

Above the din of children and nurse, Delia Dutton made
herself heard. "If you *please*, Sir Giles, your trunks have
been placed in here." She led the way to a large bedchamber off the sitting-room. "And Lady Elizabeth's room
is next door," Delia continued. "The children are on the
opposite side."

Elizabeth smiled at the unknown woman. "If you think
to organise us, you are sadly out, I fear, Miss—?"

"Dutton, my lady."

"You must bear with us, Miss Dutton, for this is all quite
normal for us."

"Delia," Marie called her abigail away, "I'm sure if
they need anything, they will ring for one of the maids.
Meanwhile, if you could send down for tea and toast,
please."

Delia Dutton did as her mistress bid and left. Fannie
hugged Elizabeth before leaving to check on Lady Agatha,
and Jane and Marie promised to tell all as soon as the
newest guests were refreshed and ready.

Elizabeth leaned down to hug her young daughter and
assure her all was well and then, with a grateful look
towards the nurse, she followed her husband into the room
designated as his.

Giles turned around at her approach and reached out to
pull her into his arms. "Well, dear heart, we are here at
last."

"I hope she's truly all right," Elizabeth said as she nes-
tled her head against her husband's shoulder.

"If she's not, you shall just have to mend her as you did me, sweetheart. Meanwhile, I'll go collect your things from next door. Who was that officious woman?"

"I have no idea." Elizabeth sighed. "I am either much more tired than I realised or else there are a great many confusing things going on all at once."

Giles kissed his wife. "We shall wash our faces, change our clothes, and then march out to have our tea and toast with Jane and get to the bottom of all this," he promised.

While Giles and Elizabeth were changing, Jane and Marie peeked in on Lady Agatha and Delia joined Hetty Mapes in the kitchen, where the sounds of the hubbub all through the old house could be heard as distant echoes and the occasional slammed door.

Hetty Mapes sang tunelessly as she readied ingredients for peach pies and listened patiently to Delia Dutton's instructions.

"You did hear me, did you not?" Delia asked as Hetty continued to hum to herself.

"The saints in heaven could hear you, Miss Dutton, never you worry about that. Now you just run along and stop fussing about what the babes will be eating and all the rest. I know how to do my job, never you fear. And," she added pointedly, looking up to stare the abigail full in the face, "I'm sure you have enough of your *own* duties to keep you busy so you needn't bother yourself about mine. There must be a flock of hems that need mending and seams that need stitching and whatnot."

Delia Dutton sniffed and left the room not a moment too soon. Fannie came through the hall door as Delia disappeared up the back stairs.

Fannie looked towards the stiff receding back of the other abigail. "Good riddance," she said succinctly.

Hetty Mapes nodded and called out to June to pour Miss Fannie a spot of tea. "I thought it was only me she got on the wrong side of but if she's got you against her, the poor woman doesn't stand a chance. I've never met a person you couldn't get along with, Fannie Burns. Except the new master."

"It's not that I can't get along with him." Fannie was suddenly defensive. "It's that I've not liked his attitude since he first walked in the door."

Hetty raised her brow. "But then we didn't know who he was. I can hardly credit it. Our lady's Daniel back after all these years and years. He is a broody one, but then he was broody as a young one, I recall."

"I well remember," Fannie said darkly. "And he's not changed much."

"But for all of that, he's her ladyship's son, after all." She hesitated before adding, delicately, "And such stories the girls are telling about overhearing talk of the abbey ghost being as real as can be."

"You best not listen to gossip," Fannie said primly.

"And him here forever because of her ladyship," Hetty continued. When Fannie did not reply, Hetty spoke again. "And Major Aldworth being Lady Agatha's son, but Lady Agatha was never married to an Aldworth."

"That's enough, Hetty," Fannie said. "We may have been here at the abbey when the major was small but we weren't here when my lady was young and brokenhearted and forced to marry against her will."

"Nothing could make me think her ladyship capable of anything bad," Hetty Mapes informed Lady Agatha's abigail.

"Good. Then there's no need for gossip to wander all over the countryside and down to the village," Fannie ended, casting a hard eye at June and May, who were peeling potatoes, their eyes averted. "So the girls can just put their long ears back in their heads and have a care about hurting those who don't deserve it. Careless talk can breed trouble."

June blushed and looked up. "I'm sure I don't know what you mean, Miss Fannie."

"You'll understand me plain enough if any hurt my lady," Fannie told the maid.

"I never would!"

"Good. Her past is her past and none of your concern. I'd best get back up to her."

"I've made the macaroons she likes so much," Hetty said, turning away. "Let me get them for you to take up." Fannie waited for the biscuits and then left the kitchens and so did not see Hetty Mapes turn, arms akimbo, hands on her ample hips, to stare her two helpers straight in the eye.

"Now then," Hetty told them, "I shall speak plain. What's our business up here at the abbey isn't anybody's business anywhere else or the culprit won't be long working for me."

"I only asked Mrs. Merriweather's maid about how he came to be called Aldworth," June defended herself.

Hetty made a sound which told of her low opinion of June, Mrs. Merriweather and her maid. "You've no sense at all, June Small."

"And I got no answer," June replied. "She said her mistress couldn't make head nor tail of how Major Aldworth could be Daniel Steadford-Smyth."

"I've not said a word," young May put in. "Even about the ghost being his father."

"Hush up!" Hetty said and scowled at the young girl. "Unless you wish to be thought dicked in the nob, you'll keep such stuff to yourself."

"Have you seen him, Hetty?" May persisted.

"Seen who?" Tim asked as he came in from the back garden, his arms full of fresh cabbage.

"The abbey ghost," May said, round-eyed.

Tim deposited his burden on the long, rough-hewn kitchen table and grinned at the young maid. "If you've a mind to see the abbey ghost, I can show you a place in the spinney you have to come, but mind, it's got to be just us alone and 'tis only after dark when he makes himself seen."

May's freckled face showed her excitement, lively hazel eyes staring at him intently. "Will you take me with you, truly?"

The cook reached for her rolling pin. "Wash that cabbage, young May, and give over worrying about ghosts. Away with you, you rascal," Hetty continued to Tim. The look she gave him sent him, grinning, out the way he came while Hetty was still shaking her head. "In the spinney indeed."

"Tim says he'll show me the abbey ghost," May proclaimed as she wiped her hands and left the potatoes to June.

"You go out to the spinney, alone, in the dark, with that young jackanapes and he'll be showing you more than ghosts, my girl," Hetty said.

June giggled, adding her pennyworth about the young stableman as the much younger May made a face at her and Hetty scolded them both.

"Just keep your tongue in your head," Hetty told June, "or I shall have to remember some of your own younger days."

June sobered. "I don't know what you mean, Hetty Mapes."

"No? Well, just remember you worked here with me all those years ago when you were May's age."

"All those years ago!" June repeated, affronted. "Well, I never!"

"Nor should you," Hetty said primly, ending the conversation.

17

MARIE TIPTOED INTO Lady Agatha's bedchamber and stopped when she saw the apparition hovering near the dowager's bed. Sir Harry shimmered in the morning sunlight from the window beyond him. He turned to see who Agatha was looking at.

"Am I disturbing you?" Marie asked timidly. Her words were for Lady Agatha but her gaze kept drifting towards the apparition beside her.

"Not in the least," Agatha replied.

"You can speak for yourself," Harry said grumpily. "I, for one, have waited nearly half a century for Aggie to know I still exist and I damn well would like some time to enjoy it without someone or other forever interrupting us."

"Harry, you're scaring the poor child," Agatha told the ghost.

"I shall leave," Marie told them both. "I'm truly sorry, I didn't mean to intrude."

"No, please, don't go," Agatha called out.

Harry came towards the young girl. "You might as well stay or I'll not hear the end of it." He watched Marie shrink back and stopped where he was. "Aye," he said, talking more to himself than to the girl. "You have the look of Aggie and that's a fact. She's the spitting image of you at her age, Aggie. Well, don't just stand there like a lump. If you're my granddaughter you've surely got the spirit to stand up to a ghost or two."

"I've stood up to worse," she told him, her chin lifting bravely.

"Naught's worse than your grandfather when he's in a mood," Agatha told the girl. "Come nearer, child . . . let me see you."

Marie did as she was bid, coming to stand beside the bed which had been hers these past few months. "I can hardly credit all that has happened. My father told me but it seems so hard to believe."

"What do you mean, hard to believe?" Harry demanded. "You've seen me yourself."

"Not you," Marie said hastily, "I mean our relationship. Relationships," she amended, looking back towards the bed, where Lady Agatha sat propped up by piles of fluffy down-filled pillows. The bed covers were woven of dark reds and greens and blues, an exotic oriental design which was repeated on the walls, the floors, the drapes and even the tablecloths. "I still don't understand why my father never told me his real name. It never seemed to matter in the past but when he bought the abbey, when we came here, he knew we would meet and still he said nothing."

"You must forgive him for that, child." Agatha spoke softly and slowly. "When he left—" Her words faltered and Harry came towards the bed, concern written large upon his pale brow, his skin luminous as sunlight filtered through him.

"Aggie—" Sir Harry said.

"I'm perfectly all right, Henry."

At the definite tone in Agatha's voice, Harry retreated. He subsided to a perch at the foot of her bed, watching her with anxious eyes as she looked towards her grand-daughter.

"Marie," Agatha began, "when your father left here, he vowed never to ask another thing of his family—or what he thought was his family. I was much younger, if that is any excuse, and I thought it would be worse for him if he knew the truth of his birth. Perhaps I was sorely wrong."

"You had to make a choice and you made it," Harry put in. "There's no point in worrying over spilt blood. Milk!" he added hastily. "I meant milk."

Lady Agatha's full attention was upon Sir Harry. "You must own you were not sorry you killed my father."

"I *was* sorry. Not for him, but for us," Harry admitted. "I was born a soldier from a family of soldiers, you can't expect me to weep over the death of a selfish villain who caused you so much grief. Although I would have preferred to run through your good-for-nothing brother Nigel."

"Harry!" Agatha exclaimed.

Harry grinned. "And that's more like it, Aggie. No more Henry this and Henry that, but your own true Harry sitting here before you, ready to do your bidding."

"Ready to do my bidding."

"In an instant!"

"Then, please, keep quiet whilst I speak to my—to our— granddaughter."

Harry made a grimace and a growl escaped his throat but he said not one word.

Marie tried to ignore the shimmering form which grew alarmingly tall as he rose from the bed and stalked towards the windows, his ghostly back to the room and the two women. His hands clasped behind his shadowy back, he seemed to ignore the conversation behind him.

Lady Agatha reached for Marie's hand. "Have you met Jane yet?"

"Yes, Lady Agatha."

"Marie, I think it's past time you call me grandmother."

Quick tears welled up in Marie's dark eyes. "You don't know how much I've longed to have a family. I mean, of course, I love my father most dearly and we have been perfectly fine—just the two of us—but, still, I have often wondered what it would be like to have a proper family. I've even wished for it and now I find I do have family, but I am so confused."

"As well you should be," her grandmother told her. "But, Marie, your father is having a worse time of it, I'm sure. You see he has felt so wronged, and he was, child. He truly was. The man he thought to be his father was cruelly unkind to him and, as Daniel grew, Homer's animosity seemed to know fewer and fewer bounds. Your father was forced away and I fear he thought none here loved him. I thought it best if he were away from Homer Smyth. I thought it safest for his sanity and his safety."

Sir Harry the Ghost made a low sound in his throat from across the room. "That scurrilous cad Smyth should have been drawn and quartered," he said under his breath.

"So you sent my father away?" Marie asked quietly.

"No. He ran from us and I thwarted my husband's one and only attempt to find him. Later, I found he had joined the army. And then I was told"—she faltered—"I was told he died in battle."

"And he nearly did," Sir Harry said from the windows. "He was a right brave lad and nearly lost his life trying to save mine, I can tell you that. If I hadn't pushed him away he'd have died with me. The best son a man ever had, that's our Daniel."

Agatha stared at the form of her lover, part shadowy where he stood against the drapes, part luminous where his face reflected the November sunlight. "You were with Daniel aboard the *Victory*?"

"Yes. Aggie. And I kept him alive for you, love, as long as I could. As long as I lived, I kept him safe." Harry came back towards the bed, his long stride effortless as his feet never quite touched the floor. "And you have him home now, Aggie."

"Yes." Agatha reached out to touch Harry but he shrank back from her outstretched hand. "What's wrong?"

"Nothing," he answered, but his troubled thoughts coloured his words. "I just don't know what happens if we touch. I don't want to harm you."

"You could never harm me," Agatha said softly, her love in her eyes and her voice.

Marie watched the two of them, the elderly woman, so much older than the thirtyish ghost who looked down with such longing at his love.

Harry came as near as her next breath, longing to touch his ghostly lips to her cheek. "And well you know I could never harm you, Aggie-my-love. Nor allow any others as long as I was around to know it. I've come through death and beyond and come back to ensure you were happy and safe."

"And you've been here all this while and I could not see you, could not speak to you."

Sir Harry smiled, his handsome face lighting with the love he felt for his lady. "Ah, and such a small price that seems now that you can see me and hear me. I'd have spent centuries helping young lovers if it meant we could have even this, dear heart."

Marie was drawing away from her seat beside the bed when his words stopped her. "Helping young lovers?" she repeated.

"Aye, and that's been my penance for my misdeeds while alive," Harry admitted to his granddaughter. "To help young Steadfords attain their true loves. And I've done mighty well, if I say so myself," he added, "as Jane and her Charles and Giles and his Elizabeth can attest. Let alone the Beal girls, although I'm not sure I was supposed to do that, since they weren't Steadfords, nor did they marry Steadfords, but somehow it's all come out right, for here my Aggie is, talking to me again at last. And then there's you and your father."

Marie's forehead wrinkled into concentrated lines. "My father and I?"

"You're seeing me, aren't you?"

"Yes, of course," Marie responded.

"Well, then," the ghost said, as if he had made a telling argument. "Only lovers can see me," he told her.

"But I'm not—" Marie began and stopped in midsentence, her blushing cheeks belying her words.

Harry leaned towards the girl. "Young Hargrave can see me too," he informed her, "which should tell you something."

Marie looked towards the ghost as if he were an emissary from heaven itself. "What should that tell me?" she asked.

Harry gave his granddaughter an impatient shrug. "Why that he loves you, girl, what else? Surely he's said so."

"Well, yes, he has . . ."

Lady Agatha watched the girl closely. "And how do you feel?"

Marie looked into Lady Agatha's kindly eyes. "I think I truly love him . . . although, never having been in love before, I have no way to judge."

"Does your heart race?" Harry asked.

"Henry," Lady Agatha began, only to be stopped by a ghostly smile.

"And am I back to Henry?" he asked.

"Harry, then—"

"That's better and my question is the same." He looked back towards Marie. "If your heart races and your brain can't control its thoughts of him and you feel you'll die if you're far away from him, then it's love, girl, and best you know it early."

Marie blushed to the roots of her dark hair. "And he can see you too, which means he must feel the same," she said softly.

"Since he's already said so, there's not much surprise there, now is there?" Harry replied.

"But what of Fannie and my father?" Marie asked, the words bursting from her before she could stop them. "My father's seen you and so has Fannie."

"Aye," Harry replied.

"But, Harry," Agatha argued, "you said only lovers can see you."

"And that's been a fact for all these years, love."

"But, Fannie, surely she's an exception. She sees you because of me."

"Does she?" Harry rejoined.

Agatha thought about the question. And finally a slow smile began to form. "Are you saying Fannie and Daniel—?"

"I'm saying nothing," Harry replied. "They must speak for themselves."

A tap at the hallway door turned their attention to the opening door as first Jane and then Elizabeth and Giles trooped into the large bedchamber.

"Are we intruding?" Jane asked.

"You could never intrude," Agatha said truthfully. Her smile was wide as first Elizabeth and then Giles and Jane came near for a kiss and assurances that Lady Agatha was well.

"I'm right as rain, with all of you here," Agatha proclaimed, taking Jane's hand in her own.

"And not a word to me," Harry said darkly.

"Oh, Sir Harry." Elizabeth smiled at the apparition. "How grateful we all are to you."

"As well you should be," Harry told her. "Where would any of you be without me, I'd like to know."

"I, for one, would still be bedridden," Giles said, grinning.

"Glad you realise it," Sir Harry replied.

Marie was staring from one to another of Lady Agatha's visitors and Jane smiled at her. "Now it's Marie and Hero Hargrave's turn for your ministrations, is it?" Jane asked. She reached for Marie's hand. "I remember Hero as the most tiresome young man, given to the most awful practical jokes. I do hope he's changed," she added merrily when she saw Marie's disconcerted expression.

"My wife," Charles said from the doorway, "is not the diplomat in our family." He came forward with his elder son and his daughter. "You cannot imagine what she says to the Americans," he said easily, casting a smiling glance towards his wife. "She is probably one of the reasons they declared their blasted ridiculous war."

"Is a war ever ridiculous?" Giles asked.

"Is one ever *not* ridiculous?" Jane asked back and her husband laughed.

"My little diplomat," he teased.

Lady Agatha called to the children and asked about the others, so that Elizabeth and Jane went to fetch them as Giles and Charles and Harry watched young Charles and little Agatha come close to meet their great-grandmother. After they'd each been introduced, Marie bent to shyly kiss her grandmother's cheek.

"I think I'd best see to the housekeeping."

"Make sure your father is all right," Agatha asked and Marie promised she would.

"And the rest of you watch that you don't tire my Aggie," Harry fretted.

"We won't stay long," the duke replied.

"Nonsense," Agatha proclaimed. "Your company is the very best medicine, Charles. Come give me a kiss and tell me if Jane has told the truth in her letter about wild Indians and Frenchmen. And this is little Agatha, is it?"

"No, ma'am," the little girl said in a tiny voice. Her large eyes were as blue as a summer sky and just as wide as she sat atop the wide bed.

"You're not?"

"No, I'm big Agatha now," the child said in a self-important voice.

"You are not," her older brother challenged. "You're just turned five."

"She shall be big Agatha if she likes," Lady Agatha told him and earned a shy smile from her little namesake as Jane and Elizabeth came back with the rest of their broods.

"Oh, my." Lady Agatha reached to hug the young Becky and be introduced to the two new babies in their mothers' arms.

Jane's son squirmed off the bed, away from the three Agathas and the babies. He made for the windows, in the process walking straight through Sir Harry.

"Oh, I do say!" Sir Harry the Ghost exclaimed.

"Sorry," the duke said, grinning. "But he can't see you, you know."

"Papa, who are you talking to?" Little Agatha asked.

"It's just grown-up talk," her father replied.

"I can see where this situation could become confusing," Giles put in.

"And ticklish," Sir Harry added.

"Do you really feel it when someone walks through you?" Giles asked, bringing young Charles to look around and stare at his cousin.

"What did you say, Cousin Giles?" the boy asked.

"Of course I feel it. Wouldn't you?" the ghost asked.

"Nothing," Giles told young Charles. "I was merely thinking out loud."

Sir Harry was slowly fading away.

"Henry, are you all right?" Lady Agatha asked.

"I'll be back when there are fewer people about. It takes more effort than you can imagine to stay visible and I'm not as young as I look."

"Who is Grandma talking to, Papa?" Little Agatha asked.

"No one. It's just more grown-up talk, Aggie."

"Grown-ups sometimes amuse themselves by talking in riddles, sweetheart," Elizabeth told the child with a smile. "We are often quite silly."

"Papa!" Charles turned away from the windows. "Come look! It's snowing! Can we go out, please?"

His excitement brought the two girls scrambling off the bed and racing towards the window.

"Ah, youth," Sir Giles said and earned Lady Agatha's laughter.

"As if you youngsters knew anything about old age!"

Jane sat beside her grandmother. "You *are* feeling better, aren't you?"

"I'm feeling fit as can be."

"That's wonderful news," Elizabeth said, sitting on the opposite side. "We've been planning your birthday this age and you had us woefully worried, I can tell you. We thought we'd have to cancel your party."

"My party?" Agatha asked, looking from one to another. "What are you talking about?"

Jane answered her grandmother. "We've planned a wonderful party for you and you must gain back all your strength for it."

"If you don't, we'll ferret out the Bath chair my nurse Elizabeth forced upon me and put you into it, Lady Agatha," Giles told the matriarch.

"It's a wheeled chair?" Jane asked.

"That's a wonderful idea, dear," Elizabeth told her husband. And to Jane, she explained, "Giles was wounded in France and I was hired to nurse him back to health. He did not want to cooperate."

"Untrue," Giles defended himself.

"Papa hurt?" young Becky asked, coming to hug her father's legs.

"Papa's not hurt anymore, little one." He scooped his daughter up into his arms. "And I think it's about time we gave Grandmother a bit of rest."

Young Charles came to plead with his father. "Can we play outside, Papa?"

"Perhaps for a little while," the duke responded.

"I'm fine," Agatha protested, but one by one her visitors left, Jane lingering last to make sure there was nothing her grandmother needed.

"I don't want a fuss about my birthday, we haven't celebrated yours," Agatha said once they were alone.

"We shall celebrate together," Jane promised. She smiled as she kissed the older woman's pale forehead. "And don't fret about the weather. I've put in a special request for your birthday."

"Don't be flippant about the Good Lord, Jane," Agatha told her granddaughter as the younger woman left.

All the happy sounds of her family left with Jane; Agatha was once again alone in the opulently decorated room. She looked towards the windows, watching the snow pile up against the window panes, and suddenly the world was very cold and blanketed in white silence. A melancholy loneliness welled up within her and she almost called out Harry's name, but Fannie arrived with fresh clothing from the gatehouse.

"I wondered where you were keeping yourself all morning," Agatha told the woman who was both servant and friend.

"I've been down to the gatehouse to check on our things and see that all was right and tight. I've not been gone all that long."

"I thought perhaps you were with Daniel."

Fannie blushed scarlet. "I don't know what you mean. Whyever would I be?"

Lady Agatha watched her scarlet-faced abigail. "You were helping with the tenant books, were you not?"

"We've long since brought the accounts up to date," Fannie said. She was turned away and keeping herself busy shaking out the dresses she had brought and putting them away in the clothespress.

"I see," Agatha said.

"This terrible room," Fannie said, "I'm sure you'll be glad to see the last of it."

"Mrs. Beal did have some peculiar tastes."

"And have you seen the children?"

"Yes, Fannie, I have." Lady Agatha was amused by Fannie's flustered attempts to change the subject.

"They're outside now, playing with the Beecher girls in the snow. Young Tim said Jessie and Dulcie seem quite fascinated with the abbey. They're forever coming around and asking about the abbey ghost Becky Beal talks of in her letters, he says."

As Fannie chattered on, Lady Agatha closed her eyes and leaned back against her pillows, a small smile playing around her mouth. In the distance outside she could hear the muffled shouts of children's laughter; inside the garish room she could hear Fannie rattling on about the Beecher girls and young Jane being home and all the others. Her world seemed once again small and cosy as Fannie fed the fire and settled down to her sewing.

- 18 -

THE MORNING OF Lady Agatha's seventy-first birthday found the abbey brimming with activity from cellars to roof, and a very disgruntled ghost muttering to himself about blasted humans getting in his way no matter which way he turned. Children underfoot, maids running in and out of everywhere, Jane, Elizabeth and Marie seeing to all the last-minute details of the household and their own toilettes, was bad enough but by midday neighbours and villagers were arriving and sending Sir Harry the Ghost to the uppermost attics for a bit of peace and quiet.

Below the attics, Fannie found a gift on her bed and opened it to find a beautiful gown of apricot silk and a note saying it was hoped she would accept the gift and wear it to Lady Agatha's party. Fannie smiled at the thought of Jane's trouble, for she knew her benefactor had to be Jane. And she was more pleased than she wished to admit when she put the simple gown on and smoothed it over her generous curves. It fit as if made for her and perfectly complemented her gentle colouring. Feeling a bit foolish, Fannie took extra care with her hair, weaving an apricot riband through her curls and peering deep in the looking glass. She saw her own clear blue eyes but the rest of her seemed alien, as if some unknown lady had slipped into her skin.

Downstairs Delia was attempting to order Hetty Mapes about and was being firmly put in her place and out of the kitchen as Fannie descended the grand stairs. Upset by the insult to her dignity, Delia went in search of her mistress but found Fannie first.

"I don't know how you can abide that Mapes creature," Delia Dutton declared. "Nor do I think her cooking is good enough to make up for her manners. She has airs and graces quite beyond her place, as do many *others* in this house," she added with a telling stare at Fannie's gown.

Fannie looked amazed. "Airs and graces? Our Hetty? I don't know what you mean."

Delia sniffed. "Anyone with delicate sensibilities would." She started away and then turned back. "Miss Burns, I have been hearing some very strange tales about a ghost."

"I beg your pardon?"

"Well, I know it's ridiculous but I've heard talk of a ghost."

Fannie gave Marie's serving-woman a blank stare.

Delia stiffened. "A strange tale of a ghost that has haunted the abbey for years and years."

"Really?" Fannie asked with the air of an innocent.

"You needn't look at me as if you think me addled. Of course I know it can't be true."

"Of course not," Fannie agreed.

"But there is a *great* deal of talk," Delia persisted.

"You must know how imaginative children can be."

"But it was an adult who was speaking of seeing the ghost."

"In all probability you merely overheard an adult talking about something the children had prattled to them. Children love to make-believe. That's the danger with eavesdropping," Fannie told the woman. "You only hear part of a conversation and can completely misinterpret it."

"I was not eavesdropping," Delia said in cold accents. "And if I were you, Miss Burns, I should worry less about others eavesdropping and more about my own duties to my mistress. Lady Agatha is hardly up to such goings-on as are planned for today."

"You are quite right," Fannie replied, surprising Delia Dutton. "You *should* worry less about eavesdropping and more about your duties to your mistress."

Delia stiffened her back, her head held high as she pointedly ignored Fannie and marched off down the hall towards the great oak stairs that led to the upper regions of the huge abbey. She got no farther than to the entrance hall when she was engulfed by arriving guests and enlisted in helping them dispose of their cloaks and outerwear.

Young May was busy sweeping up the tracked-in snow, Jane was hugging old acquaintances and introducing Marie to the Beechers as Letty Merriweather arrived with Margaret and Charlotte Summerville and Captain Tompkins.

The newcomers were escorted into the front parlour and the long unused ballroom, which were already half-filled with villagers and near neighbours.

The sounds of celebration carried up the stairwell to the chamber where Fannie was helping Lady Agatha dress.

"I don't see the point in denying the truth," Agatha was saying as Fannie assisted her into a rather old-fashioned gown made of bottle-green velvet. "Since the Dutton woman is living here she is bound to find out about Henry."

"She's a mean-spirited, prune-faced meddler and she'll never see him for herself, that's a certainty," Fannie replied.

"I always liked this dress," Lady Agatha said, changing the subject.

Fannie obliged her mistress by following suit. "Squire Lyme and Eleanor were arriving as I came up the stairs and the Beechers were already here. And of course young Hero was early and dancing attendance on our Marie."

"Our Marie," Agatha repeated, pleased. "We have a great many blessings to be thankful for. Jane and her family home with us, and Giles and Marie and, of course, Daniel," Agatha added, watching her serving-woman.

"I don't know why you've been giving me such strange looks these past days," Fannie said.

"I think you know very well," her mistress replied.

Before Fannie could reply, Giles and Daniel arrived with the Bath chair for Lady Agatha. They assisted her into the chair and then escorted her down to her birthday party, Fannie beside them supervising every move. At the top of the stairs Charles came forward to lift Agatha from the chair and carry her down. Sir Giles and Will Carston manhandled the large cane-backed chair down the wide stairs. Daniel directed their progress and Fannie came behind, watching the man who was Lady Agatha's son until he glanced in her direction. Then she swiftly turned her attention towards her mistress and ignored his dark-eyed gaze.

"Carefully, now," Fannie cautioned Charles as he placed Lady Agatha back into the chair once they reached the front hall.

"Don't worry so," Jane reassured Fannie. "My husband is terribly large but he can be remarkably gentle."

"Thank you," Charles said as he placed Lady Agatha's shawl about her and reached down to kiss her forehead.

"Lady Agatha!" Leticia Merriweather cried. She came forward towards the small group already around Agatha's chair. "How wonderful to see you up and about. We have all been so very worried."

"You can stop your worrying, Letty," Agatha replied tartly. "As you can see, there's nothing wrong with me that a bit of rest won't fix."

"Well, of course there's not," Letty replied a bit too heartily.

"Shall we go in?" Marie suggested.

"I'll steer this contraption for you, shall I?" Giles said as he stepped behind the chair.

"I'll just tell everyone you're on the way," Letty said and bustled ahead of the small group to announce Lady Agatha's arrival.

Tables heaped with all the delicacies Hetty Mapes was famous for lined two sides of the abbey ballroom, and a string quartet played softly at the far end of the large room.

"Here she is, everyone," Letty cried as Lady Agatha appeared in the doorway surrounded by her family and Fannie. The children skipped forward, racing to meet the Beecher children and head to the cake trays.

Cries of "happy birthday" accompanied Lady Agatha's progress around the room as she was wheeled slowly forward to greet her well-wishers and accept their words and their gifts.

"Come now," she said, overcome as more and more gifts were proffered. "This is much too much fuss."

"This is exactly right," Jane said, smiling at Hero Hargrave. He stepped forward and gave a deep bow to Lady Agatha before he pulled Marie aside to meet his parents.

"Papa?" Marie reached for her father's arm. "Will you meet the Hargraves?"

"I suppose I shall have to, sooner or later," Daniel told his daughter with a wry smile. He followed Marie and Hero across the room to where the elder Hargraves were seated, as Jane's young Agatha scrambled up onto Lady Agatha's lap.

"Aggie—"

"I want to ride with Grandmama."

"It's all right, Jane," her grandmother said. "She's light as a feather and she'll be good as gold. Won't you, Agatha?"

"Yes, Grandmama," little Aggie promised solemnly and clung to her grandmother as a score of strangers came near to pay their respects.

Fannie drifted off towards the tables, checking on the maids and going back to the kitchens to see if Hetty needed any help.

Daniel, talking with the Hargraves, saw her depart and made his excuses a moment later, following her out. The hall beyond the noisy party was empty, the green baize door to the kitchens just falling shut. Daniel hesitated and in that moment Delia Dutton came flying out from the servants' hallway, breathless and very much upset.

"Major Aldworth," Delia cried, "I must speak to you at once."

Daniel masked his impatience. "Yes?"

"In private, if you please." She marched forward towards the door to the library, Daniel following her and closing the door.

"What is it?" he asked as soon as they were inside.

"I'm sorry, Major, but it's come to this. It's her or me."

Daniel stared at the woman. "What are you talking about?"

"I am talking of leaving your service, sir," Delia said dramatically. "I've been with you for over fifteen years, but I shall not stay one day longer unless you rid this house of that woman."

"What woman?"

"Fannie Burns!"

It took Daniel a moment to respond. "Miss Burns is Lady Agatha's abigail."

"I am well aware of that fact and I've made allowances for her interference in every aspect of this house and its workings but she has just spoken to me in the most disparaging and humiliating way in front of the kitchen staff."

"What did she say?"

"She spoke of my interfering where I did not belong, as if she were not doing that very thing. As if *I* were not in charge of this household!"

"You are not in charge of this household," he told her. "I am. You were in charge of my daughter's care and her household when we were apart."

Delia Dutton looked affronted but she stuck to her purpose. "Nevertheless, I have taken all I can bear. Either that woman goes or I do."

"I am sorry to hear that. I am sure Marie will miss your help since she and Mr. Hargrave are to be married and she and Hero will live at the abbey."

It took Delia a moment to digest his words. "You—you are telling me *I* am to go? I cannot believe you would side with Lady Agatha's servant over myself!"

"I have no choice," Daniel told her. "And I can well understand why you must leave. With bad feeling between you and my future wife, you would be most uncomfortable in my house. I shall make provisions for your future."

"Your—you are *marrying* her?" Delia was shocked speechless. "Well, I assure you, I shall not stay where I am not welcome."

"I take it this interview is at an end?"

"Yes! I shall pack." Delia drew herself to her full height, glared at her erstwhile employer and sailed to the library door.

In the hallway Delia nearly bumped into Fannie.

"Congratulations!" Delia spat the word at Fannie as she sailed past. "I shall be packed and gone by morning!" She gave a ferocious glare past Fannie's shoulder and left.

Fannie stared after the other woman, and turned to see Daniel standing in the doorway behind her.

"Whatever is wrong with that woman?" Fannie asked.

"Please come inside," Daniel said. He turned back into the library and stood inside, waiting until Fannie came to a stop before him. "Miss Dutton is leaving my employ."

"I've not thought much of her, but I never thought she would simply pack up and leave without notice," Fannie replied. "Nor do I know why she would congratulate me."

"She was congratulating you upon our upcoming nuptials."

"What nonsense are you nattering on about?"

"I remember you as such a shy, quiet creature," he said, smiling.

"You are demented!" Fannie cried.

"Haven't I asked you to marry me yet?"

"No, you have not!"

"Well, I am now, Fannie Rose Burns."

Fannie stared at the man, a hundred thoughts tumbling around inside her head. Lady Agatha's long lost son had just asked her to marry him—that made no sense. She had been sixteen the year he ran away; she remembered the dark-haired man as a sulky, silent boy. Now he was home.

"Fannie Rose?"

"You can't be serious."

"But I am."

"How dare you wander about telling people we're to wed?" Fannie was rewarded by a frown, a look of unsureness clouding his dark eyes.

"Are you saying you do not return my affection?" Daniel asked hesitantly.

"It's good to see you a little less sure of yourself, Major Aldworth. And of me."

"You've not answered me, Fannie Rose." Watching her changing expressions, he could see something in the blue of her eyes which tried to search out his secrets. Surprise was fading, a softening look meeting his own gaze. "What would you do if I kissed you, Fannie Rose?"

"I'd slap you for being too familiar," she told him.

"Would you slap me very hard?" he asked softly.

"Yes . . ."

"You do not sound very positive, Fannie Rose."

She looked up at him, her eyes unable to leave his as he began, slowly, to lean forward.

"What are you doing?" she asked softly.

"You had better slap me, Fannie Rose," Daniel said as his lips came down to meet hers.

Fannie's astonishment turned to bewilderment and then to wonder as Daniel took possession of her lips, his arms reaching to draw her closer. Her arms seemed to have a will of their own as they reached around his neck, her shy reactions warming in his embrace.

"I must say it's about time." Sir Harry the Ghost was rather pleased by their reactions as they sprang apart, looking around the room like guilty schoolchildren. He eyed his son with lifted eyebrow but as he was invisible at the time none could see it. "I thought you'd never come up to scratch."

"We were not aware you were here," Daniel said.

"Invisibility is one of the few blessings of ghosthood."

"It may seem a blessing to you but it's damnably disconcerting for the rest of us," Daniel said grumpily.

"Daniel, you should show more respect to your father," Fannie said.

The object of her advice turned back towards her and smiled. "Ah, at last."

"At last what?"

"You've called me by my name," he told her. "But you've not answered me yet."

Fannie tried not to smile. "Nor can I without your mother's permission."

Daniel grabbed Fannie's hand. "Then we shall find her and ask her blessing this instant." He was already pulling Fannie with him towards the door.

"She's with her guests," Fannie protested.

"The more the merrier," Daniel proclaimed as he marched her forward.

The sounds of the party in the ballroom filled the corridors, people laughing and talking over the music from the string quartet. A group of squealing children raced out of the ballroom and down the hall past Daniel and Fannie.

"I should see to the children—"

"They have nursemaids for that," Daniel said, still holding her hand and propelling her forward.

As they entered the ballroom they nearly ran head first into Captain Tompkins.

"Aldworth! Egad, it is you! And after all these years. Good to see you, old man!"

"And you," Daniel said as he tried to pass on by, his hand still firmly holding Fannie's.

"Come away from this crush," Tommy Tompkins said. "I've found a bit of solitary bliss in the parlour beyond and we can have a cigar and talk of the Spanish campaign. Why I remember in aught eight when old Nappy drove us back to Coruña. 'Gad, those blasted snow-bound hills, as if we were back home, remember? And slipping away in the night but the ships weren't in harbour. What a debacle. And then the horrible crossing with those contrary winds—"

"Daniel," Fannie put in quietly.

"Yes, yes," Daniel said to them both, stopping the flow of the captain's voice. "We must talk later, Tommy. Meanwhile I must find my mother."

"Didn't know she was here, laddy. Sorry." Before he could finish speaking Daniel was away, pulling Fannie with him towards where Lady Agatha was surrounded by family and friends. Jane looked up from handing a plate to her grandmother as her uncle and Fannie came forward.

"This is not the time," Fannie was protesting as they reached Lady Agatha's side.

"Not the time for what?" Marie asked as she and Hero joined the small group around Lady Agatha's chair.

"Ah, Marie, good," Daniel said. "I'm glad you're here because I must talk to Lady Agatha. And your Miss Dutton is even now packing. She will be gone by morning."

"Gone by morning?" Marie was astounded. "Papa, whatever can have happened?"

"She cannot abide my intended wife."

"Your—" Marie started and stopped.

"Uncle Daniel." Jane clapped her hands together. "I had no idea. Where is she?"

"Standing beside me," Daniel said. The small, startled group around Lady Agatha heard him continue: "That is, if her employer will allow her to say yes. I am positive my mother will be able to persuade her employer to give her blessing."

"Daniel, are you serious?" Agatha asked.

"Yes, Mother."

Lady Agatha looked up towards the blushing Fannie. "In all our years together, I could never imagine you leaving my employ, for I could never think of losing your company." She smiled. "I'm glad I shan't have to."

"But Grandmother, you don't seem surprised," Marie put in.

"Nor should you be, since Fannie and your father both have seen"—she looked around the room—"our friend," she ended cautiously.

"By Jove," Hero put in, "she's right and I never gave it a thought."

"What I want to know," Jane said, smiling at Fannie, "is how long this has been going on."

"Nothing's been going on," Fannie said, blushing.

"From the very first day Fannie Rose came to help me with the household accounts and told me to go to the devil," Daniel responded.

"You didn't!" Lady Agatha interjected.

"After all, I didn't know he was your son," Fannie defended. "Besides, he seemed perfectly dreadful."

"And now?" Daniel asked.

"Maybe a bit less dreadful," Fannie teased.

"You do love me!" Daniel nearly shouted.

Letty Merriweather turned from her conversation with Captain Tompkins in time to see Major Aldworth pull

Fannie into his arms. A surprised assemblage watched as he kissed her soundly.

"Upon my word!" Letty exclaimed. She dragged the captain with her as she crowded near Lady Agatha to hear what was going on. "Lady Agatha, whatever does this mean?"

"You'll have to ask them," Lady Agatha said, letting the others give the news. She looked towards Fannie. "I think I'd best rest now. For a little while."

Fannie moved quickly to take possession of the wheeled chair and guide it backwards, Agatha smiling at those nearby who wished her well as she was wheeled out of the room.

Charles came behind them, reaching to lift Agatha from the chair and carry her up the stairs. Fannie hurried ahead to open the door to her chamber and fussed about as Charles deposited Lady Agatha on the bed and kissed her before straightening up.

"I'll go back down and help keep the hounds at bay," he promised. "When you're rested and want to come back down, just give a call."

"Thank you, Charles," Agatha said. Fannie was arranging the pillows and bedclothes around her as the duke left. "Are you happy, Fannie?"

Fannie stopped her work and looked down at her friend and employer. "Aggie, it seems as if I am dreaming. But it is a wonderful dream."

"Good," Lady Agatha responded. She sighed contentedly. "I think I'll just nap a bit."

"You aren't feeling ill, are you?" Fannie worried.

"A little rest and I'll be fine," Lady Agatha promised as she closed her eyes. "Just fine."

LADY AGATHA WOKE slowly from her dreams, the sounds of her birthday party below distant and vague. A light snow was falling, her thoughts going to the well-wishers below who would have to travel home through the worsening weather.

"They really should be leaving," she said out loud.

"Do you wish them gone, Aggie?" Sir Harry asked. He came closer to the bed.

"I didn't see you," she told him, her eyes lighting with love as she watched him come forward. "You look so handsome, Henry. Just as you used to. Why do you look so worried?"

"I fear you feel unwell."

"I'm just so tired. I think I'll doze for a while longer before going back down."

Her eyes closed as she spoke. Jane came in to find her grandmother asleep and Sir Harry hovering over her.

"Is anything amiss?" Jane whispered.

Sir Harry looked up and Jane could see the concern in his eyes. "I do not know. She seems very weak."

Jane's brow furrowed with worry. "I'll tell my uncle."

The room was silent again when Jane left, until Agatha woke again.

"Harry? Are you here?"

"I'm here, my love."

"How? How can you be here?"

"Because I love you. I always have and I always shall."

"Why then did you not stop my brother?"

"I couldn't, Aggie. They had the law in their favour and you were already wed. All I could offer you was dishonour and shame."

"And happiness . . ." Her eyes suddenly flew open. "Harry!"

"Yes, love."

"What is happening to me? I feel so very strange and tingly."

Sir Harry came nearer, his love in his eyes as he gazed down at the woman he'd love through life and death. "You soon have a choice to make, Aggie. You must decide whether you wish to stay here, with me, or go back, at least for a while, with the others."

"I don't understand. What do you mean, stay here or go?"

"Aggie, you're speaking to me and your lips aren't moving, love. You're with me now, for a few moments, so that you can make a decision. If you decide to go back, we will be apart, Aggie, since my debt is now finally paid in full. I must leave here."

"Leave? To go where?"

Sir Harry smiled gently. "To go—forward. It is your decision to make, sweetheart, and you cannot make a wrong one. If we are together you will find your Evelyn and in time the others will join us. If you stay, you will be with our Daniel, who was lost to both of us for so very long and with your grandchildren who love you and want you close."

Lady Agatha's eyes drooped closed. "So tired . . ." she said again.

"Then sleep, my love, sleep and rest while I say my good-byes."

Sir Harry waited until she was well and truly asleep before he straightened from her side and disappeared through the wall. He floated down through the ballroom ceiling and hovered, unseen, above the merry throng. In a group of well-wishers, near the string quartet and a table heaped with quince tarts and candied fruit, he found his quarry.

He drifted down behind Letty Merriweather and Margaret Summerville, so much to his son's surprise that Daniel blurted out his question before he thought. "Is she worse?"

Margaret Summerville, who was in the midst of a discourse on the wonders of her son-in-law elect, the Marquess of Longworth, stopped and stared at the major. "Is who worse, Major Aldworth?"

"You'd best come," Harry replied, unheard by any but Daniel and Fannie.

"I'll go to her," Fannie said.

"I beg your pardon?" Margaret Summerville said, her attention turning towards Fannie.

"There's no need, yet," Sir Harry told her. "But I'd like to speak to Daniel alone for a moment."

"In the library?" Daniel asked. "I shall leave directly."

"And I," Fannie said, "will run up and see to my lady. If you will excuse us," she said with a distracted smile towards the two women.

"My apologies," Daniel said as he escorted his intended wife across the room and away from Letty Merriweather's and Margaret Summerville's questioning gazes.

Margaret looked at Letty. "Did I say something amiss?"

Letty's frown grew. "I seem to have missed a chapter," she said. "For I haven't a clue as to what has just transpired."

Charlotte Summerville, coming up beside her mother, heard their conversation and shrugged her pretty shoulders. "If you ask me, there's no sense in the entire family," she said.

While Fannie went up to Lady Agatha's bedchamber, Daniel closed the library door and turned to face the ghost of his father.

"It is serious, is it not?" Daniel asked.

"With your mother? I think so, Daniel. But that is not why I asked to see you. I wished to say—" Sir Harry sighed. "I wished to say so many things to you and now that I've the chance, by God, I'm not sure how. You know I was proud of you."

"Yes, sir."

"Well, I still am. Proud of you, I mean. Proud of who you've become." Harry found the words hard and quickly went on. "And now at last you know your mother loved you too, loved you past endurance and to her lifelong agony at what happened to you."

Daniel swallowed hard, his voice ragged when he answered. "I know many things now I did not know before."

"And that's a shame, but there it is, and we must make the best of what we're given. All of us. If I had it to do over again, I'd have held my temper that long ago night and perhaps you'd have had the life you should have had. But the past is past and none can change that. I've come to say good-bye and to tell you that I—I love you—and I always have. Always will."

"You're saying good-bye?" Daniel asked.

"I've fulfilled my penance and it's long past time, my boy. Long past time for me to be on my way."

"And—my mother?"

Harry hesitated. "I've no answer. That's partly her decision and partly the Good Lord's and none of it mine."

"I understand, sir. And—I thank you for all you've done for me and for Marie. If not for you, God knows how I would have ended up. You gave me more than your fortune, sir. You gave me back a belief in human kindness. In love."

"Which you seem to be using in full measure today," Sir Harry told his son.

Daniel smiled then. "Yes, sir, it seems I am."

"Good. A man needs a good wife or his life is worth little. I know," Harry told his son.

Daniel nodded slowly, his eyes straining to see the slowly dissolving apparition. "Don't go yet, we've barely had a chance to meet again."

"I cannot stay. But we will be together again, I promise you. I'll not be here much longer. I would embrace you if I could, Daniel, for you're a son any man would be proud of, but I cannot touch the living. Just know I shall be waiting for you all."

"I know that now, sir . . . Father . . ." Daniel added as his father faded from view.

In the bedchamber above Fannie and Jane bent near Lady Agatha.

"Should we send for the doctor?" Jane asked Fannie.

"I'm not sure," Fannie replied.

"Stuff and nonsense," Lady Agatha told them both. "I'm fit as a fiddle."

"She looks so peaceful," Fannie continued. "Asleep like that."

"Asleep? And can you not hear me?" Agatha asked even as she realised they could not. "You cannot hear me," she repeated in awe. "How very strange."

"It's not so strange, love," Sir Harry said.

"Harry—I didn't see you there."

Harry Aldworth reached out his hand to his love. Agatha stared at it and then, slowly, reached forward. Their hands met, a shock going through them both.

"Ah, Aggie-my-love," Harry said. "How I've longed to touch you. Hold you near."

Agatha smiled at him. "And you said we could not touch. You see how wrong you were?"

"Aye, and we could not touch. Then."

Lady Agatha turned to look at Fannie's and Jane's concerned faces. "They do not seem to realise I'm awake. Or to hear us."

"Nay, Aggie, they cannot. They have not the ears to hear our whispers."

"Am I dead, then?" Agatha asked.

"No, love. But if you wish to go back, you must wake to them now."

Agatha smiled at her lover. "I don't want to go back, Harry. I want to go on. With you . . . But it's been so very long and we make a strange pair, since I've aged and you've not. I don't know why you wish to have me still, but I wish to be with you. If you'll have me."

"Oh, Aggie-my-love, you're my own true beauty and always were. Always will be. Come towards me now, love."

He reached out and Agatha stretched out her own arms towards him.

"Harry—look at my arms! They're those of a girl."

"Come and see the rest of you," Harry said.

Agatha let Harry draw her to her feet. She looked back once, to see Fannie and Jane leaning over the bed where her very own figure seemed to lie.

"How strange to see myself there when I am truly here."

"Aye, and more strangeness to come. Come and look in the mirror."

"I no longer look in mirrors," Agatha told the love of her life.

"Just this once, then. For me. Soon you won't be able to."

"And how do I say no to you?" she asked. She let him draw her forward until she stood in front of the looking glass across the room. Her eyes widened and then she gasped. "Why, it's not me!"

"Aye, but it is you, the you of eighteen, when first we were together. Enjoy it, my dear, you shall soon start to fade from the looking glass and then will see no more in mirrors."

Agatha looked back once more. "But Harry, they are so unhappy. I left so quickly, I didn't realise. I should go back to say proper good-byes."

"They'll not be able to hear your good-byes now, nor mine. They must live out their own lives, Aggie, as we did. And we are at last free."

"Free . . ."

"Yes, sweetheart, free at last. Come away, come away with me, Aggie-my-love. Look away now," he added as he saw her looking back at the elderly body on the bed.

She did turn then, turned towards him and smiled. "Where shall we go?"

"We shall have the honeymoon we never had, my love. We shall dance on rainbows and love throughout eternity, my own true loving girl," Sir Harry said with a loving smile.

"Dance on rainbows . . ." Aggie repeated as her body and then her voice slowly faded.

"How strange," she said, looking down at her own hands. "I almost cannot see them."

"You soon will see them in an entirely different way, sweetheart." Harry spoke with knowledge that he knew was true and yet had not known before that very instant. "Come away now and let the living have their time here."

"Harry—kiss me," Agatha demanded.

Harry reached for his love and brought her near, his arms somehow as strong as she remembered. He bent his dark head and captured her lips, hearts together as their bodies disappeared, their souls united forever.

"Fannie?" Daniel asked from the doorway as he entered Lady Agatha's bedchamber. "How is she?" He came forward, Charles just behind him. Elizabeth and Giles shooed the children back into the hall and closed the door after Marie and Hero slipped inside.

Fannie turned a tearstained face toward her future husband. "She's gone. Oh, Daniel, she's gone. . . ."

Daniel reached to hold Fannie, trying to assuage her grief.

"Janey, are you all right?" the duke asked his wife.

Jane still held her grandmother's hand. With tearstained cheeks she looked up and smiled through her tears. "She is happy. I know that."

"We'd best tell the guests," Marie said in faltering accents, and then broke down in tears against Hero's shoulder.

"Oh, Marie, no!" Jane broke in and came around the bed where Lady Agatha lay to reach for her cousin's hands. "No, none of that! She is with her love at last."

"But how do you know that?" Marie cried.

"We can prove it, if you like. We shall shout out for Sir Harry high and low and you will soon see he is with our beloved Gram. And Marie, they are happy at long, long last."

"Jane," Sir Giles said softly. "That is a wonderful sentiment but you can hardly prove it, you know. Even if we don't find Sir Harry. He's never come round merely because we wished it. Only at his own discretion."

Jane stared at Giles. And slowly regained her smile. "Ah, but I *can* prove it."

"How?"

"Come along, all of you," she said as she headed towards the door and the hallway and stairs beyond. The others came behind, crowding out into the hall and then watching as she picked up her skirt and began to run up the stairs. Halfway up, she turned to look back. The tears still streaming down her cheeks, she was smiling. "Well, come along, then. If you need proof, I have it."

One by one, first Charles, then Marie and Hero, then Giles and Elizabeth, and finally Daniel and Fannie, followed Jane up the stairs.

Jane waited for them all at the door to the attics, leading them up the final flight until they stood in the attic, the high round window letting in the late afternoon light.

Jane sped to an ancient trunk and undid its fastenings. "Charles, Fannie, come near—you will have to explain to the others."

"Explain what?" Marie asked.

Jane threw the trunk open and the others peered inside.

"But nothing is there," Daniel said.

"Exactly!" Jane said, triumphant. She looked up at Charles and then at Fannie. "And which of you wish to tell the others?"

"Tell us what?"

Fannie spoke. "Lady Agatha's red ball gown . . . the one from her portrait in the Long Gallery. It's gone. It was here," she added. "But it's—gone."

"Didn't I tell you?" Jane said, tears sparkling in her eyes but a peacefulness in her gaze and a smile playing around her mouth. "It was so special to them and she would need it now, for she couldn't go off to eternity dressed in elderly garb—not when her Harry was so elegant and young."

"But what does it mean?" Marie cried.

Jane reached for her cousin's hands. "Oh, Marie, don't you see? It means Grandmother is young again. As young as she was when she and Sir Harry first fell in love. And it means—wherever she is—she is dancing."

459

ACCLAIMED AUTHOR OF THE NATIONAL
BESTSELLER *DESERT SUNRISE*

CALICO

Raine Cantrell

Maggie vowed to open the New Mexico
mines she inherited and run them as well as
any man. Especially McCready, the one
man who stood in her way. He was a
thieving scoundrel, a land-hungry snake
who could cheat the sun from the sky. She
despised him—and yet she was bound to him
in a stormy marriage of convenience. And
McCready was determined to win this battle
of the sexes. But first he had to tame the
wildest heart in the West...

___1-55773-913-7/$4.99